P9-CAD-498

DISNEP

# DUMBO

## CIRCUS OF DREAMS

DISNEP PRESS

LOS ANGELES • NEW YORK

Copyright © 2019 Disney Enterprises, Inc.
All rights reserved. Published by Disney Press, an imprint of Disney Book Group. No part of this book may be reproduced or transmitted in any form or by any means, electronic or mechanical, including photocopying, recording, or by any information storage and retrieval system, without written permission from the publisher. For information address Disney Press, 1200 Grand Central Avenue, Glendale, California 91201.

Printed in the United States of America
First Hardcover Edition, February 2019

1 3 5 7 9 10 8 6 4 2

FAC-020093-18362

Library of Congress Control Number: 2018953267

ISBN 978-1-368-02763-2

Designed by Gegham Vardanyan

disneybooks.com

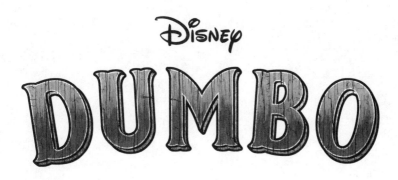

# DISNEY
# DUMBO

## CIRCUS OF DREAMS

By Kari Sutherland
Screenplay by Ehren Kruger

DISNEY PRESS
LOS ANGELES · NEW YORK

# PROLOGUE
## MISSOURI, 1919

welve-year-old Milly Farrier leaned against the grimy window of the train's passenger car as it rolled through the plains of whichever state they were in now. If she squinted, the yellow grasses, clusters of emerald trees, and occasional farmhouses all swirled together—almost like one of her mother's abstract paintings.

Of course, Max Medici, the circus director, had always made Annie Farrier stick to a more relatable style for the boxcar signs and fairground banners. Not too abstract, but not too realistic. No, he wouldn't want that to destroy the magic of the experience. Only Milly, Joe, and their father had gotten to appreciate the sweep of colors her mother had brushed onto canvas in what she called her "action" pieces. They captured what the audience and circus lights looked like to her as she hung upside down from a horse during the show, wind whipping through her hair.

Milly knew he tried his best, but the new ads Rongo slapped together could never match her mother's bold, *eye-catching scenes. Milly's stomach twisted and a tear slid down her cheek as she clutched the key dangling from her necklace.*

*A door in the ceiling screeched open and her younger brother dropped down into the car. She'd told him countless times not to cross between the train cars unless the train was at a standstill, but the eight-year-old never listened.*

*Quickly, Milly wiped her face dry. She had to be strong for him now.*

*"Joe, you know you're not supposed to change cars while we're moving—" Milly scolded.*

*"Unless it's an emergency," Joe finished as he got to her row. "But it is an emergency! Guess what, guess what?" Joe bounced onto the wooden bench across from her. His floppy brown hair bobbed lightly, and his smile was so wide it could have split the sky. It was nice to see him so happy.*

*"What?"*

*"We got a letter! From Dad!"*

*Milly's heart nearly stopped, but Joe kept going, his words clattering almost as fast as the train's wheels. "It was jumbled up in Mr. Medici's accounting mail at the last station, and he just found it." Beaming, Joe reached into his jacket and pulled out a stained white envelope with a flourish.*

*Milly resisted the urge to lunge for it. Joe handed it over and she tugged out the creased paper, her eyes drinking up her father's loose handwriting. As she read the words, Joe babbled on.*

*"He's coming home, Milly! The army's released him with a medal and everything. Mr. Medici already sent off a telegram telling him to meet us in Joplin."*

*Tears of joy pricked her eyes as she smiled up at Joe.*

*"He's coming home," she echoed in wonder.*

*"I can't wait to hear all his stories," Joe said. "I know he couldn't put anything in the letters in case they fell into enemy hands, but I'll bet he is a hero! Thundering onto the battlefield. I bet the Germans just threw up their hands in surrender. . . ."*

*Milly's mind drifted, her brother's chattering fading into the background, just like the swaying of the train. She clutched the letter to her chest as though she could grab hold of her dad through his words. But she'd be able to hug him soon enough. Just a little bit longer. He'd make everything all right. Milly knew he couldn't bring back her mother—nobody could do that—but her dad was strong, her dad was brave, and he could do just about anything else.*

*They wouldn't have to worry anymore. He'd take care of everything. He'd take care of them.*

# CHAPTER
# ONE

ith a squeal of brakes, the train shuddered backward to the edge of the tracks, dead-ending on the side of a wide meadow. Joe whooped loudly as his body was flung into the air, only one hand anchoring him to the pole at the back of the caboose. Then the jolt of the stop slammed him back onto the porch, his shoes sliding across the floorboards.

Milly wouldn't approve. She'd scold him for being reckless. Her forehead would get that wrinkle in the middle that had never been there before Mama died. But Milly wasn't there to see.

"Yeehaw!" Joe shouted as he leapt from the train.

They were finally there: Joplin, Missouri, where his dad would meet them any day now.

Across the meadow, several boys his age raced toward him, waving madly. Joe raised his hat in return. Well, not *his* hat; it was his dad's and a bit too large for him, truth be told, but the other boys couldn't see that from this far away.

*Shhhboom.* Boxcar doors slid open down the line and the circus crew hopped out in a well-rehearsed dance, one of them staying behind in each car to toss down the supplies. The faded white-and-red-striped fabrics and poles for the tents came out first, along with the fence to keep out those seeking a free peek.

"Hiya, Joe," Rongo called. The strongman hefted a stack of boards that weighed significantly more than the fake inflatable barbells he wielded onstage.

"Hi, Rongo." Joe waved as he ducked under a roll two men were lugging toward the field.

"Get to your own post," Rufus Sorghum spat at him.

Joe gave the grouchy roustabout a cheeky salute, then scampered off to where Milly was already sliding crates down a ramp. In the boxcar behind her, Catherine the Greater, the magician's assistant and wife, was carefully sorting more. There were a lot of boxes.

The meadow might have been peaceful and empty now, but before nightfall a border fence would encircle a village of tents, with the animal enclosures set up as far from the fence as possible. Medici didn't want Joplin's citizens dodging entrance fees to view the creatures.

"Oh, good, you're here," Milly said. "Let's get these over—"

"Have you seen Barrymore?" a frantic voice called.

"Oh, no," Milly said, exchanging an amused grimace with Joe as Catherine came to the doorway to see what the fuss was about. Puck, another one of the performers, sounded panicky.

"He must have gotten loose again," Joe said. He sidled toward the next car. "You know, I can get under the cars and up on top, look for him in all the tight spaces he loves. . . ."

Milly sighed. "Fine, go find the monkey."

Joe was off before she'd finished the sentence.

"Just get back here as soon as you do!" she called after her brother. Shaking her head, she continued stacking boxes of streamers and lights in a pile.

"I'm not the fortune-teller, but I predict he'll return precisely as the final box is unloaded," Catherine said, a smile playing on her lips.

"Wouldn't have it any other way," Milly answered, with a grin of her own.

The main tent always went up first, followed by the surrounding exhibitions. Last were the behind-the-scenes living areas. It was strange to be back on solid ground after a week on the rumbling train, but Milly was looking forward to some quiet time. It was ten times easier to measure chemicals precisely when the floor wasn't shaking under her.

"Thank you, Milly." Ivan the Wonderful, the magician, patted her head as he passed her to collect a box.

By late afternoon, the camp was taking shape, and they'd started on the living quarters tucked at the back. Joe returned after a long hunt (Barrymore had hidden inside a feed bag, demolishing half the peanuts) and helped Milly spread out their tent.

"Here, let me," Ivan said. He strode over and lifted one of the main poles easily, setting it into the small hole Joe had dug while Milly looped the fabric over the next pole. Once the first was secured in the ground, they lifted the second and third. Joe tacked the ends into the ground as Milly carted in their belongings from the boxcar.

"You can always stay in our tent, you know,"

Catherine said, her hand resting on Milly's arm as they crossed paths by the train.

"I know," Milly answered. Ivan and Catherine were incredibly kind and did everything they could for her and Joe. Every day they asked if the kids needed anything, such as help sewing extra cloth onto Milly's sleeves to make them longer. Sometimes they would bring little gifts, like a bag of cherries they'd bought at a train station along the way. And every night, they slept nearby. At the first stop after their mother died, Milly and Joe had squeezed into Ivan and Catherine's tent, but it was cramped and claustrophobic. Milly couldn't set up experiments without Ivan tripping over them, and Joe's early rising woke Catherine, who was a light sleeper.

"We're okay," Milly said. "And we know you're right next door if we need anything. Thank you, though."

"All right, then. Don't hesitate." Catherine smiled and continued on her way.

When Milly reached the tents, Ivan and Joe were carrying the cots in. Ducking inside, a thrill ran through her. There'd be three this time instead of two—finally, their family would be reunited. Together, they brought in the mattresses and laid them out so that nobody would have to climb over anybody else to get outside.

The delicious smell of stew filled the air. Joe's stomach gurgled loudly.

"Ha!" Ivan laughed. "All right, *niños*, I think that's a good stopping point."

Summoned by the aromas of beef and carrots, the troupe filtered into the meal circle. This was the true heart of the circus. Usually Medici would be walking among them, checking on everyone, but Milly didn't see him anywhere. Maybe he was visiting the animals instead. He'd been particularly obsessed with their newest elephant lately. Milly and Joe grabbed bowls and stood in line with Ivan behind Miss Atlantis, the resident mermaid.

"Good clear night, isn't it?" Ivan asked, gazing skyward.

"A bit muggy for me." Miss Atlantis fanned herself.

"Did you get everything unloaded all right? Need a hand?" Ivan offered.

"Oh, I'm all set, thank you."

Milly wasn't surprised—Miss Atlantis almost never accepted help, claiming she didn't want to be a bother.

The mermaid twisted her torso, stretching her back muscles. "I'm looking forward to sleeping on steady ground, though. I need to get my sea legs!"

After they dished up, Milly and Joe followed Ivan

to where Catherine had saved them all spots, staking out two coveted stools for her and her husband. Sitting cross-legged on a mat next to her was Pramesh, the snake charmer, and his nephew, Arav. Milly was disappointed to see they'd left their snakes in their quarters tonight. She liked studying them . . . as long as they were far from her mice, that is. Pramesh nodded in greeting, his face wrinkling with a smile. Arav, still shy and reserved even after years with the circus, ducked his head. The kids sat on the ground beside Pramesh, slurping up the delicious stew.

"Puck is a genius. He really is," Joe declared.

"I think you'd be happy with anyone's cooking," Milly teased, "as long as you didn't have to lift a ladle."

"Not true. The week that Rongo was in charge was . . . um . . ."

"Yes?" a voice growled from behind them.

Milly and Joe turned to see the strongman looming over them. His dark skin contrasted with his bright yellow shirt, and the sparkle in his eyes glinted in the moonlight.

"Go on, Joe. My week was . . . ?"

"Unconventional?" Joe said. "But maybe it was just too heavy on the pepper for me."

Rongo chuckled and winked at the kids. "I may or

may not have done that on purpose." Milly suddenly remembered Medici's having gotten terrible indigestion that week. "I wasn't hired on as a cook. I'm just as glad as you that Puck handles it all now. Speaking of, I'm going to grab a second helping."

\* \* \*

After dinner, they all gathered around a warm fire. Milly fiddled with the key on her necklace as she and Joe leaned against Catherine's and Ivan's legs. Under the twinkling stars, the campfire stories began. This was Milly's favorite part of the day. The jobs and chores were done, and everyone relaxed and laughed— even if the nights had become more subdued and the stories more wistful than celebratory. It was still nice to look up at the sky and listen to the rumble of voices, the old tales and worn-out jokes. Puck picked up his concertina and pressed it in and out slowly, the music a sweet underlay to it all. The crowd called for Miss Atlantis to sing, and finally, after much cajoling, she chimed in with her rich, beautiful voice. Milly swayed appreciatively.

"Well, I must go check on Tanak," Pramesh said once the song was finished, rising in one fluid motion.

Pramesh doted on his python, catching rats for

it at every stop. At least he made sure it was always either draped around his shoulders or securely contained. Milly would be crushed if it somehow got to her mice.

"He's asleep," Pramesh whispered, gesturing toward Joe.

Ivan craned his head to see. "Well, it's been a long day, and you know how he likes to get up early."

Milly groaned. "Yes, we do. Ivan, do you mind?"

Without a word, he slipped his arms around Joe and lifted him up. Milly went around the circle, saying her good nights before following him back to her tent.

"*Buenas noches*, little ones," Ivan said as he tucked Joe's blanket around him. "Sleep well." He dropped a kiss on Milly's forehead before ducking out into the night.

* * *

"Holt will be here soon," Catherine said as Ivan rejoined her at the fire.

Leaning his shoulder against hers, Ivan nodded. "Let's hope the war hasn't broken his spirit. Those kids need him whole." They'd both seen plenty of soldiers with haunted eyes attend their shows. Not even the clown act could break through to them.

"Yes, let us hope."

The fire crackled and bowls clanged as the crew set them in the washbasin. Miss Atlantis nodded good night to everyone as they left, her arms submerged in soapy water. Puck did all the cooking, so she had volunteered for washup. They'd need to use the dishes again in the morning for breakfast.

A circus life was cyclical, that was for sure.

# MISS ATLANTIS
## BOSTON, MASSACHUSETTS, 1913

*enny Davenport sighed as her mother paraded another would-be suitor around the house, showing off every imported trinket from Japan—the delicate fans, the porcelain teacups and jade statuettes. All tiny, all extremely breakable and dainty. Why was her mother so obsessed with qualities the exact opposite of Penny's?*

*Not that Penny didn't try to be dainty. She had trained her feet to take miniscule steps, kept her arms tucked in close at all times, and hardly dared to breathe in the formal sitting room. Even now, her corset squeezed her lungs uncomfortably. What if she fainted? Would the gentleman rush to her aid? She'd probably wind up squashing the man; he was reed-thin.*

*Penny snorted, then ducked her head. Mrs. Davenport shot her a scathing look, but kept up her prattle about the imported saucers.*

*Considering his fascination with the gold inlay, her latest would-be suitor, Jonathan Billings III, would not even notice if Penny collapsed. Her shoulders slumped.*

*That was nothing new. Nobody seemed to notice her except her mother, and she only did so to list off all the things Penny was doing wrong.*

*Why did she even have to be there? Neither Mrs. Davenport nor Mr. Billings cared if she was present. Penny's mother was making a case for Penny's worthiness as a match using everything else in the house.*

*Penny shifted, the satin of her dress crinkling loudly.*

*Jonathan Billings III turned, his eyes landing on her for only the second time that evening. "And you, Penny, I assume you embroider. Are any of these yours?" He gestured to the hand-stitched miniature pillows, fit only for a mouse's head.*

*Penny rose from the settee. "I'm afraid not, sir. I have no skill with the needle. If you'll excuse me, please, I'm feeling rather tired."*

*Mrs. Augustine Davenport reeled as though Penny had slapped her. Jonathan Billings III blinked rapidly.*

*At least he was looking at her for a change.*

*"May you have a lovely night, sir," Penny said, dropping into her best curtsy. She may not know how to sew—her fingers could never quite grasp the needle right—but she could at least curtsy. Of course, she ruined her exit by banging her thigh into the armchair, the vibration shaking the room. Penny silently cursed her clumsiness. Her mother would be up later to chastise*

*her for her unladylike deportment, but by then it would be too late. Jonathan Billings III would be long gone, another potential fiancé scared off.*

If I met someone on my own terms, would it feel different? *Penny wondered.* Maybe if I sang to them, they'd actually look at me, not the shiny room around us. Maybe if we had something—anything—in common . . . *She knew most men were only interested in her wealth.*

*Up in her room, Penny wriggled free of her dress and ripped at the stays of her corset until it was loose enough for her to actually breathe. Throwing a robe around her shoulders, she sat at her mirror and began brushing her hair, tugging at the long, dark tresses.*

*Without even thinking about it, she began to sing, notes cascading out of her, the music lifting her spirits.*

Tap, tap. *She just caught the sound at her door as she paused between songs. It was too soon for her mother to have extricated herself from the embarrassment below, not that she'd knock in any case.*

*"Come in, Helen," Penny called.*

*A cautiously optimistic face poked in, and then the maid entered, carrying a tray of biscuits and milk.*

*"I thought you might like some refreshments, Miss Penny, since you didn't have much of an appetite during Mr. Billings's visit."*

Penny smiled as she sat up and moved to the table and chair by the window. "It's true, I'm always nervous during these meetings. Thank you, Helen."

As Penny dipped a biscuit in the milk and took a bite, she watched Helen tidy the room and turn down the bed. Penny often felt a stab of guilt as Helen did these menial tasks that Penny was perfectly qualified to do. Helen was up before dawn, stoking fires, scrubbing floors, chopping food, and doing whatever other task was called for that moment. She probably hadn't sat all day.

"Why don't you get off your feet for a minute?" Penny gestured at the spare chair in the corner.

Helen shook her head and kept fluffing the pillows. "No, thank you, miss. This is just the last bit before I turn in for the night. I'll be resting soon enough."

Penny could hear the rumble of voices beneath them. She thought about her mother tutting at her all day, reminding her to sit up straight or commenting on how sloppy her needlepoint was—as if that even mattered. Lately every conversation turned into her mother trying to coerce her into a marriage of convenience. "I wish I could please her." Penny sighed.

"She has a high bar, miss," Helen agreed.

"Yesterday she told me I was a poor excuse for a lady and was better suited for a circus. She actually called me a freak." Penny's heart squeezed, remembering the *disgust in her mother's eyes. All because Penny couldn't embroider in as tight a line as she could.*

*"Oh, my lady, I'm sure she didn't mean it." Helen smoothed down the coverlet, then met Penny's eyes. The maid's eyebrows quirked up as she tried to lighten Penny's mood. "Can you imagine—you, in a circus?"*

*Penny smiled. "You don't think I would make a lovely magician's assistant?" she joked.*

*Helen laughed and waved off the possibility, but something turned over in Penny's mind. Was that idea so preposterous? She'd always loved when the circus came to town. The last time she'd been truly happy and relaxed with her parents was years ago, when they'd taken her to one. Fingers sticky from sugary treats, and dazzled by the music and lights, she had raced around, her parents following along indulgently.*

*Maybe a circus troupe would be more forgiving of her flaws. She'd also get to travel, more than if she were married to some financier. She'd get to meet all kinds of interesting people and collect memories rather than trinkets for the mantelpiece. Shaking her head, she finished her milk and got ready for bed. If she were fast enough, she could pretend to be asleep before her mother barged in to scold her on yet another failure as a daughter.*

*Once Helen had left her and Penny settled into bed, she allowed herself to sink back into what-ifs. If not the*

23

*circus, maybe there was something else she could do—somewhere else she could go? But any relative would just cart her back to her mother. If she joined the circus, then even if her mother did track her down, she'd never ask her to return. She'd be too affronted. She'd probably spin some story of how Penny had caught pneumonia and perished rather than allow anything to tarnish the Davenport name.*

*Penny would need some savings, as only the top-billed performers lived comfortably. She'd also need an act. Hmmm. Her voice was strong—that was one set of lessons she had enjoyed—but most circuses didn't feature singers. Penny turned on her side, and her gaze caught on her bookshelf, where Hans Christian Andersen's collected fairy tales jutted out from among the other titles.*

*If Penny really wanted to cut ties with her family and upbringing, start fresh in a new world, wasn't she like the little mermaid? Striving for something all her own? A new identity? It wouldn't be a quest for love, though—quite the opposite: she'd be trying to escape the stuffy men and arranged marriages of her esteemed social circle.*

*But just like the little mermaid, who hadn't felt right in her scales and longed for human legs, no matter what she might have to suffer to get them, Penny was willing to make some sacrifices. She knew circus life wasn't easy;*

*living on the road couldn't be, and she'd lose the comforts of her station. But that was a small price for the chance to be more herself. To move as she liked, without fear of destroying anything in a room full of ridiculously fragile tea sets. Nobody to tell her to walk more softly or she'd rattle them off their shelves. Nobody to try to squeeze the air out of her with a corset made for a younger Mrs. Davenport. "If it fit me at your age, it should fit you. . . ."* her mother had said.

*Maybe she could present herself as the voice of those whom legend believed to be lost to the sea—the citizens of Atlantis. She had secretly hoped they'd transformed into mermaids ever since first reading of the tragic fall of their empire in Ignatius L. Donnelly's* Atlantis: The Antediluvian World. *Why not? If people could traverse snow and ice to reach the bottom of the world, who was to say the ancient Atlanteans hadn't figured out a way to survive underwater?*

*Penny fell into a restless sleep filled with dreams of mermaids and rolling country landscapes and brightly lit stages. And when the Medici Bros. Circus arrived in town two months later, she took the plunge.*

*She dove from the tight-lipped, tight-minded upper crust into the welcoming arms of a band of misfits, and she never looked back. No matter how low the circus's fortunes became. Not even when she ran out of savings,*

25

*spending the last she had on medicine and blankets for her troupe. Her new family was worth it. And though she still couldn't always shake her self-consciousness, they never judged her or made her feel inadequate. She was free to be whoever she wanted. And that was . . . Miss Atlantis.*

# CHAPTER
# TWO

illy turned to her final patient, stethoscope at the ready. She listened carefully, then pulled the tubes out of her ears with a satisfied nod.

"Breathing normal, heart rate normal. You are cleared to perform!" Smiling, she set the mouse back inside its cage. He squeaked up at her, then tugged at the edge of his red ringmaster suit, almost as though he were adjusting it.

Milly giggled. Timothy Q. was the most outgoing of the mouse trio, which was why he got to be the ringmaster in the "Greatest LITTLE Show on Earth!" His bossiness was also a factor—he was always chattering at his siblings, telling them what to do and where to go. Kids loved the miniature circus. It might not have been the biggest money earner in the Medici show, but Milly was proud of it.

Picking up her notebook, she dutifully recorded Timothy's health stats. A scientist (or doctor) needed to keep accurate data.

"Milly!" Joe cried out as he catapulted into their small tent. His sides were heaving.

As soon as she saw his face, she knew.

"Another train!" he announced triumphantly.

Milly leapt to her feet and the two kids flew through the tent flap. In the distance, they could see the smoke from the approaching train, and a long, shrill whistle blasted the morning air.

"*Niños!*" Ivan shouted as Milly and Joe barreled past the magician and his wife in the middle of rehearsal. "Wait! We're coming, too."

Ivan hurried to free Catherine from the split box, but the children didn't slow down.

The Joplin train platform was crowded with people in their finest. Several locals drew away from Joe's dirt-stained hands as he pushed through the throng, but others were too focused on the sleek black train that had just pulled in.

Soldiers poured out of the carriages to find their loved ones, tears of joy glistening on everyone's faces. Milly and Joe peered through the crowd as Ivan and Catherine joined them.

*Where is he?* Milly felt a knot of anxiety in her chest. What if there'd been a mistake? What if he wasn't coming home yet?

A woman in an enormous emerald green hat let out a squeal as a young soldier picked her up and spun her in a circle. As he set her down and stepped back, Milly saw her father, Holt Farrier, emerge beyond them.

"Dad!" Milly and Joe shouted together. They surged forward.

He hadn't shaved in a day or two, but his face was just as handsome as Milly remembered, his back maybe not quite as straight. But he was carrying a bag on his left shoulder, so perhaps it was heavy. Then he suddenly crashed to the ground, the bag sliding away from him.

Milly started.

Where his left arm should have been was just . . . air. His uniform sleeve had been pinned up neatly under his shoulder, as though the army couldn't allow sloppiness, not even for a missing limb.

Beside her Joe gasped, pausing just feet away from

their father, who appeared to have fainted. As Ivan and Catherine came up behind them, their father stirred.

His beautiful blue eyes blinked open and his gaze slowly focused on them.

He scanned their shocked faces, then mustered an empty smile as he staggered to his feet.

"I meant to tell you—in the letter," Holt said, nodding toward the space where his arm should've been. His voice was raspy from disuse. "I just didn't know how." When the kids didn't move, he gestured them closer with his one remaining hand. "C'mere. Hey, it's me."

"Is the fighting all done? Did we really win?" Joe asked tentatively.

"The country did. A lot of good men didn't." Holt's eyes grew distant, and then he focused back on his son, a glow of pride lighting his face. "Look at you, growing like a weed. C'mon, you remember me, dontcha?"

This time Joe didn't hesitate. He flung himself at his dad, who tucked him in close and then turned to Milly. Her brown hair was longer, woven into two braids, and she was wearing a jumpsuit he didn't recognize, gray with pink cuffs.

"And you—you're just as pretty as your mom."

Sadness spread over his face. "I'm so sorry that I wasn't here."

Milly nodded, her fingers moving of their own will to the key she wore around her neck. "So was she," she said softly.

Her father turned away, his eyes brimming. She moved to his left, fitting herself into the empty space at his side and wrapping her arms around his still-solid frame.

"We missed you," she added.

"Missed you, too," Holt said. He gazed down at his kids, wishing with all his heart he could have been with them, with Annie. And wishing that he knew what to do now. Raising his face to the other performers, he nodded. "Ivan, Catherine. Thank you for looking out for them."

"Of course, Captain Farrier," Ivan said.

"It's Holt. Just Holt," he replied firmly. His cavalry days were over now. He spotted the colorful sprawl of the circus in the distance. "Don't worry," he whispered to his kids. "Everything's gonna be like it was before."

Maybe things couldn't be exactly as they were before—not without Annie. But Holt owed it to his kids and the circus to try. He'd spent long nights in the hospital and long days journeying home, all the while thinking up new tricks he could perform one-handed.

As they entered the camp, things seemed the same at first. The sideshow booths and food stalls were still laid out around the main tent like flower petals, only now they were spread out, many missing altogether. Signs for the menagerie directed visitors to the back so they'd have to walk past all the other delights. And, of course, the main attraction—the Big Top tent— rose above everything like a palace. But somehow, it seemed smaller. Of course, it wasn't; it had the same red-and-white striped fabric as always. Holt was the one who'd changed.

Troupe members hurried over as word of Holt's return passed like a wave through the camp. But their joy drooped at the sight of him. Holt awkwardly tried to duck his left shoulder, as though that would make a difference.

Pramesh stepped to the front, embracing Holt tightly.

"The very best journey: the road that leads home. Welcome home!" he cried. The large python wrapped around the snake charmer's neck slid forward onto Holt.

"Uhh, no hugs!" Holt told the snake as he wriggled away from them both. "Pramesh, I missed you, too.

32

But what's going on? Camp's half the size it used to be."

"Hard times, my friend. For everyone." Pramesh shook his head sadly. The snake coiled around his neck, its tongue flicking out in agreement.

"Aaaaaargh!" An enraged yell broke the moment. The caboose door flung open and a barrel-shaped man emerged, his ruby velvet robe flapping around his ankles. Dark brown eyes glared out at the staff from under two bushy eyebrows and a dramatic top hat.

"Attention, you hapless harebrains," the man bellowed. "Why is rule number one *called* rule number one? Because *'keep the cages locked'* is the most important rule there is!"

The circus director peeled back his robe to show them the claw mark ripped across his shirt. At that moment, a small monkey face popped out of the lid of the top hat, grinning at the audience.

Muffled laughter ran through the crowd as Max Medici continued to rail, oblivious to Barrymore's presence. Miss Atlantis hid her smile behind her hand, but Catherine giggled openly and Pramesh's eyes were twinkling merrily. Puck was the only one who looked nervous, shifting from foot to foot and scratching the back of his neck. The organ-grinder was responsible for Barrymore, after all.

"And when I find that fugitive scalawag who woke

me from my nap—" Medici cut himself off, as his troupe clearly wasn't taking this seriously. "Rongo!"

"Yes, Max?" Rongo asked calmly, stepping forward.

"Who's heading camp management?"

"I'm the strongman." Rongo's voice was droll.

"Yes, and we're all wearing multiple hats." Medici tore off his own hat, but the monkey swiftly transferred to the back of his robe. Medici spun, but didn't spot him.

Turning, Medici pointed a stern finger at Rongo, ignoring the clowns, who were doubled over in laughter. "You're in charge of accounting *and* budgets *and* inventory, and that means animal whereabouts. I want you to track down that monkey."

Rongo eyed the mischievous Barrymore. The monkey had hopped down and was scurrying into a box Puck held open for him behind Medici's back. "I'll have a look around."

"Okay, back to work, everyone," Medici proclaimed, setting his hat back on his head. The circus director stopped, his eyes widening. "Holt?"

Holt nodded, a genuine smile on his face as he took in the familiar hubbub and banter, and Medici happily beckoned him up into the caboose. Milly and Joe trailed after their father into the small office.

As Medici settled into the chair behind his cluttered desk, the Farriers perched on stools.

"This winter the influenza hit us like a hurricane. Natalya, Vincenzo, the Vanderjees . . . and then poor Annie. She fought hard." Medici tugged out a dusty handkerchief and dabbed at his eyes. "She was the best of us, Holt."

Determined not to let his emotions get the better of him, Holt straightened his shoulders. "I know. So to honor her, let's have our best season yet. Now, where are my horses?"

"Ah, funny story about that." Medici leaned back, steepling his fingers over his stomach, his gaze traveling to the ceiling.

"Funny how?" Holt asked.

"He sold them," Milly and Joe piped up in unison.

Holt stared at them. They had to be joking. But Medici wasn't denying it. Holt pinned Medici with a disbelieving stare.

Medici shifted uncomfortably, reluctantly meeting his gaze. "You were off fighting Kaiser Wilhelm. Lord knows I've been busy, too—battling radio and motion pictures. There used to be a hundred traveling circuses; now we're among the very last."

"Our act was the soul of this show!" Holt exclaimed.

"And first we lost you, and then Annie, to ride them. If only Milly had learned the trade—"

"I don't want to be a show-off in your circus," Milly said firmly. "Riding sidesaddle, juggling plates—" Her father turned to study her, trying to hide his hurt.

"See, she's still impossible." Medici shrugged.

Milly lifted her chin. "I want to make scientific discoveries. I want to be noticed for my mind."

"Then learn clairvoyance or telepathy! Something I can use!" Medici waved his arms.

Joe interrupted the familiar argument. "I can do a handstand for almost ten seconds," he cut in.

"'Child Does Handstand.' We'll be bankrupt by July," Medici said.

"All those hours teaching you to ride," Holt began, staring at Milly.

"No, really, Dad, watch!" Joe leapt up and turned onto his hands, but he toppled over almost instantly. Sliding closer to the wall, he tried again.

"I love him, Holt," Medici muttered as they watched Joe collapse in a tangle of limbs. "But he did not get your athlete genes."

Holt turned back to Medici, his eyebrows furrowed.

"Hang on, without horses, what the heck is my act? I can still *ride*," he insisted. He instinctively tried to lift his arms and found himself raising only the one. He was doing those types of things a lot lately. Attempting to shrug it off, he continued. "We may have to forget the rope tricks, but the barrel jumps, speed runs . . . I had some ideas for new spins. . . ." His voice trailed off at Medici's dubious expression. "The crowds come to see *me*."

Medici looked away. "Ah, Holt, my friend, I'm afraid equestrian acts have lost their shine. People know horses—they see them every day. They want something new from a circus."

"Max, please," Holt said softly. "I need to work." Medici had always treated his troupe like family, so Holt knew he wouldn't kick him to the curb just because the horses were gone . . . but Holt *needed* to feel useful. He needed the distraction.

"Aha, good news," Medici replied. "I have one job opening."

Holt perked up. "Okay then. Give me a show-stopper."

Medici scratched his nose. His chair creaked as he leaned forward. "That old rascal Itchy McPhee finally ran off with the bearded lady. I've had roustabouts filling in since then, but I need someone to tend to the elephants."

"You're not serious." Holt couldn't hide his dismay.

Milly and Joe shared a worried glance.

"Occasionally, I am. It's a big job. You know it is," Medici proclaimed.

"No, it's just a big shovel for a big pile of—"

"Dad!" Milly and Joe scolded. Annie had never allowed foul language.

Holt staggered to his feet. "You sold my horses, but you kept your elephants. Your scrawny, mangy, cut-rate *elephants*!"

Medici held out a placating hand. "They're important. Especially this season. It goes against my nature, but for once, I have made an investment." He smiled calmly up at Holt.

Holt's shoulders sank. There really was no other option—the circus was family, home, and job all rolled into one. He had no other trade. He couldn't leave; he had to support his kids. He glanced at their hopeful faces.

"All right. Let's go see this *investment* of yours," he grumbled.

# CHAPTER
## THREE

oe hurried to keep up with Holt, Medici, and Milly, who strode toward the animal boxcars. From up ahead, they heard a loud bellow of protest. Medici sped up.

Rufus Sorghum stood at the bottom of a metal ramp, a pole in his hand. Inside the boxcar, one of his lackeys tried to corral an elephant onto the ramp, while another tugged on a rope looped around its neck. The elephant's trunk shot up and it bellowed again. Joe recognized it as Goliath.

"Let's go. Move yer ugly stinking wrinkles!" Rufus shouted, poking the elephant's rump from the safety of the ground.

A burst of anger flared in Joe's chest.

Medici scurried over, but his voice was placating. "Handle with care, Rufus. *Respecto, respecto.*"

The taller man scowled at him. "Needs to earn my respect. And don't gimme that Italian royalty act, Gustavo. You grew up shining shoes."

"Why's he calling Max 'Gustavo'?" Joe whispered to Milly as the men coaxed the elephant down the ramp to join its brother, Zeppelin, in line.

"I don't know," she answered, shrugging. "Maybe he got kicked in the head."

Rufus's eyes landed on Holt and he smirked unpleasantly.

"Well, look who's back. Or most of him," he drawled.

Joe started forward, but Milly's hand stopped him. Their dad didn't even flinch. Joe admired his confidence.

"Still glad you served your country instead of helping us sell tickets?" Rufus asked.

With a flick of its tail, the elephant splattered Rufus with mud—at least it *looked* like mud—as it lumbered past him. Rufus cursed. *Nope, not mud,* Joe realized happily.

Grinning, Joe followed Medici, his dad, and his sister, glancing over his shoulder briefly at Rufus, whose cheeks and forehead were turning pink from rage. As Rufus wiped his face, he caught Joe watching and glared at him. Joe didn't care. Rufus could glare all he wanted—Joe's dad was home now, and soon the elephants would be safe from the roustabout. Still, Joe hurried to catch up.

* * *

"As you see," Medici said quietly as he led Holt to the next boxcar, "I've been making do. But you, Holt, you know animals. And they love you!"

Holt scratched his head. He'd never handled an elephant before. He knew they were smart, and they certainly tended to pick up tricks fast . . . but would they respond to him?

Medici rolled back the boxcar door and headed inside. Hay covered the floorboards, and a large gray elephant lay on the ground. Her eyes followed them, but she didn't even bother to lift her head more than a foot off the hay.

"Voilà!" Medici exclaimed. "Meet Mrs. Jumbo. Our brand-new Asian female I bought from Brugelbecker in Biloxi. Talked him way down on the price."

Holt didn't know much about the beasts, but this one looked ill. Her abdomen was swollen, perhaps with a tumor.

She let out a tired wheeze.

"I saw something special in her eyes," Medici continued.

*Maybe your eyes were clouded by dollar signs,* Holt thought. Medici was a good leader for the most part, but he sometimes let his ambition get the best of him. Aloud, he said, "This is your investment? An old, sick elephant?"

Medici shook his head. "Oh, no. She isn't sick. Any day now, she's having a *baby*." His voice was reverent. Milly and Joe seemed to share his excitement. Their faces shone as they gazed at the mother-to-be.

"A baby?" Holt asked. "How exactly is that going to keep the circus afloat?"

"Let me show you." Medici grinned, gesturing them out of the car. Mrs. Jumbo slumped back into the hay as they left with a relieved snuffle.

Medici strode toward a nearby tent. "What's the one thing that unites all the people of the world? What brings a smile to their faces, a tear to their eyes, a hippity-hop to their hopeful hearts?"

Holt raised an eyebrow. When Medici went into performance mode—which was most of the time—he was a bit over-the-top.

"Ice cream?" Joe offered hopefully. He'd been pestering Medici to find a way to sell the delicacy for years.

Medici shook his head. "Babies!"

He flung open the tent flap to reveal a giant hay-lined bassinet, complete with a barbell-sized rattle, a massive pacifier, and a teddy bear. A banner draped overhead read WELCOME TO OUR DEAR BABY JUMBO!

"People love babies," Medici continued, striding over to the bassinet. He tweaked the lace-covered hood. "I don't, myself, but I'm the exception to the rule. People love cute things; that's why they have children. And children love small things; that's why they like babies. So . . . babies mean children mean parents mean tickets!"

Medici paraded around the larger-than-life nursery, past several plain stacking blocks, then turned to Holt, beaming. "That means big things for you and me! Pending pachyderm gender, of course, we'll paint."

Joe wandered toward several cans of paint stacked in a corner.

"You want me to babysit an elephant." Holt's expression was flat. He couldn't believe this was happening to him.

"Twenty-five cents extra for a peek in the tent." Medici bounced on his toes, mentally collecting the fares.

Holt's face darkened. "You want *me*. To babysit. An elephant," he repeated.

Medici looked ruffled for the first time. He leaned toward Milly and Joe. "Why's he saying things twice? Is that 'cause of the war?" he whispered.

That was it. Holt stormed over to Medici, his fist clenched. "I had eighteen beautiful horses!" He flung his arm out as though directing imaginary steeds around the ring.

"Yes, you did," Medici answered calmly. He tilted his head, a firm but sympathetic look in his eyes. "And a wife. And an arm. A fellow can go broke from all that living in the past."

Holt glared. Maybe there was no turning back time. That didn't mean he had to accept the present, though.

"Cha-cha-cha-ching!" Medici thrust the giant rattle into Holt's hand with a jangling sound. Having delivered the news, he sauntered away. "You'll thank me later. Elephants are the way of the future!"

"Come on, Dad." Joe tugged on his shirt. "Let's get you settled before dinner."

Holt set down the rattle and followed his kids to the living quarters. People called out greetings and he waved back vaguely, barely registering Arav meditating outside his tent or Ivan and Catherine fiddling with their one-way mirror box. Not even the rowdy group of clowns, a family from Greece, roughhousing in the campfire ring broke through his daze.

Joe and Milly ducked inside a small beige tent, a quarter the size of their old one. *Where are they going?* A spike of concern pierced the fog in Holt's mind as he entered the tent.

Three cots were crammed in next to two large trunks, one emblazoned with STALLION STARS in golden letters. A small crate formed a makeshift bookshelf, and a second crate in the corner held an assortment of pots and pans.

"Watch, Dad, I'm getting better," Joe said, picking up a handful of apples and starting to juggle them. He lunged for them as they plopped to the ground.

"Whoa, hang on, *this* is our tent?" Holt stared around in dismay. "But we had furniture, beds, rooms . . ." As the stars of the show, he and Annie had the finest, largest tent, with curtains partitioning it into two bedrooms and a main space. Holt eyed the cots nervously—he wasn't even sure one could hold his weight.

*What* didn't *Max sell?* he wondered. Panicking, he dove for the STALLION STARS trunk and flung it open. Glass tubes and colorful cups lay on top.

"Toys? What's with all these?" He lifted out what looked like a funnel.

"They're not toys," Milly said. "They're for my science experiments." She frowned—her dad was looking at them like they were from outer space. *He's going to call my studying science silly, just like Medici,* she thought. Her mother had at least tried to understand, buying her the chemistry sets from stops along the way before she had gotten sick.

With a wan smile, Holt eased onto the cot. Setting the funnel down, he took Milly's hand in his own and drew her closer. "We're a circus, darlin'. A circus. We need to be practical if we want to survive." He paused. "You couldn't take up one act? Tumbling? Tightrope?"

Milly stiffened. "Maybe I don't need the world staring at me. Maybe I'm just not you and Mama."

Holt's mouth pursed and he stood up, insulted. "Who makes the rules in this family?"

"Mama," Joe said automatically.

A silence hung in the air, fraught with tension. Annie flashed through their minds, bubbly, sweet, firm, and alive.

"Well, well—I make them now," Holt finally sputtered. "Just go to your room."

"This is my room. This is all our rooms," Milly said. She jutted her chin in the air.

Plucking his cowboy hat off a coatrack, Holt shoved it onto his head, then stalked back to the trunk. From the bottom, he hauled out a silver saddle. At least Medici hadn't sold *that*.

"You see this? You know what this is? Your inheritance." With a huff, he marched out of the tent, clutching the saddle with his arm.

"Dad, wait! Where are you going?" Joe raced to the flap and peered out.

"Don't worry," Milly said as she joined him. They watched their dad pace one way and then the other. He finally stopped next to a log and slung the saddle down atop it before straddling it, his back to them. "He's not going anywhere. He's stuck. Just like you and me."

# THE STALLION STARS
## THE MIDWEST, 1900-1914

orn and raised on a ranch, Holt Farrier could tell which horses would be steady and reliable and which would just as soon kick you in the teeth as let you put a saddle on them. It was the latter ones he loved to work with—winning their trust, teaching them he was a leader worth following. Horses Holt could understand. People . . . people were harder. He was a straight talker, and sometimes people said things they didn't mean or tried to trick him. So while he was friendly with strangers, he only trusted his small circle of friends.

Annie, on the other hand, could charm the hat right off the grouchiest rancher, which is just what she did when she met Holt at a rodeo. She raced her mare through the barrel course, leaping and turning as though they were one instead of two. Annie knew how to handle horses just as well as Holt. And crowds. She loved the roar of applause, the gasps as her horse reared on command, hooves pawing the air.

*At the end of her turn, she trotted over to the sidelines where Holt stood, eyes fixed on her.*

*"Howdy, cowboy," Annie said. "Enjoy the show?"*

*"Not bad," Holt said.*

*Annie raised an eyebrow. "Let's see you do better."*

*Laughing, Holt held up the schedule. "I ain't up for another half hour. Do you want to grab something to drink while we wait?"*

*The rest, as they say, was history. After Annie and Holt were married, they continued in the rodeo circuit for a few years. But when Medici approached them to join his circus, they jumped at the chance. They got to design their own act—the two of them—from beginning to end, and they were able to include more tricks than the rodeo judges allowed. Plus, once they had Milly and Joe, they were able to travel as a family, all together, and there was always someone to mind the babes while they were performing.*

*"Ladies and gentlemen, boys and girls," Medici's voice boomed one night in Lexington, Kentucky, "prepare to be amazed at the unbelievable feats and dazzled by the dancing hoofwork of the king and queen of horses, Holt and Annie Farrier—our very own Stallion Stars!"*

*Eight-year-old Milly peered out from the side curtain of the ring as Joe squirmed next to her. It wasn't until their parents galloped out that he stilled, his head poking through the gap under her.*

*Annie and Holt steered their horses in opposite directions through an obstacle course of hay bales, barrels, and upside-down buckets stacked in a pyramid. As their horses neared each other, Annie stood, arms flung out to the sides.*

*Joe gasped as, with a light push-off from her own steed, Annie flipped and twisted through the air, landing behind Holt. Then Holt swung sideways in one direction as Annie lunged in the other, making the horse appear to be riderless.*

*Whooping, they both pulled themselves back up while a stagehand loosed the next pair of horses into the ring. Annie slid onto one, grabbing the reins for the second. Then she stood, one foot upon each horse's back, guiding them around the ring at a canter.*

*Meanwhile, Holt showed off his rope work by swinging lasso after lasso as the rest of the herd joined the loose horse in the ring. Soon Holt had a line of horses standing together. Annie leapt back to her original horse, and together the duo directed the other horses through jumps and run patterns with whistles and called commands. Then, for the grand finale, Annie and Holt each rode their horses over the course, thundering through it with ease. The horses all galloped into a perfect spiral with Annie and Holt at the center, standing atop their saddles, arms around each other and waving at the crowd, their faces alight with adrenaline.*

*As soon as the duo was out of the ring and the horses were handed off to the crew, Annie jogged over to her kids and swept them up into a hug, the key necklace she wore bumping into Milly's chest.*

*"How are my little good luck charms?" she said, planting kisses on their cheeks. "I love you so much! Did you like the show?"*

*"Sha-baam!" Joe replied.*

*"You've been spending time with Ivan and Catherine again, haven't you?" Holt laughed as he joined them. He ruffled the tops of his kids' heads.*

*"You were great! As always," Milly said.*

*"I think we may need to add some new rope tricks," Holt said to Annie. "Maybe you could jump over a rope I throw?"*

*"Stop fiddling with the show," Annie answered. Then she smiled at her husband, her eyes softening. "We can think about it later. Right now, let's get these little rascals to sleep. It's way past their bedtime."*

*Holt scooped Milly up as Annie carried Joe.*

*"Not sleepy," Joe objected, even as he curled into his mother's neck, eyes drooping.*

*After they'd tucked the children in, Annie and Holt sat outside, gazing at the stars. The music of the circus continued in the background, but the crowd was dwindling now that the main performance was over. There'd be stragglers, of course, some staying past midnight to gawk at Pramesh and his snakes or try to tug on the bearded lady's facial hair. Boy, would they get in trouble for that!*

*"They're growing up so fast," Annie said.*

*Holt startled. He'd been thinking through the show again. "The kids? Isn't that what they're supposed to do?"*

*"Yes, I just . . . sometimes wish I could slow it all down, capture a moment—like a photograph, you know?"*

*"Photographs are pricey," Holt said.*

*"Ah, my darling, but the only thing worth anything in this world is love."*

*Holt tugged his wife to his side and she leaned her head on his shoulder. "Well, then, we must be millionaires."*

*"As rich as the number of stars in the sky," Annie whispered.*

*"And anyway, time ain't going to stop for the likes of us."*

*"You're right. Time may not stand still, but each new moment lets us learn and change and grow our love."*

*"Speaking of change—" Holt started.*

*Annie slapped his chest lightly. "Holt Farrier, are you going to be talking about switching up our act again? Haven't we already fiddled with it four times since we left Atlanta?"*

*"Well . . ." Holt didn't know what to say.*

*"You and Milly, always experimenting, exploring new things. What am I going to do with you?" Smiling, she examined him. "All right, cowboy, tell me your idea."*

*So Holt laid out his plans as Annie rested against his side, gazing at the stars. Somewhere in his speech, he figured out she'd fallen asleep, so he lifted her into his arms and carried her to their tent. There'd be time enough tomorrow.*

*A few years later, war broke out. Proud to serve his country, Holt had enlisted in the army, and although Annie fretted over him, he'd waved off her fears. Holt had never considered she would be the first one to run out of tomorrows.*

# CHAPTER FOUR

he sun peeked over the horizon, lighting the sky with orange and pink hues. Joe stooped to pick up the apples he'd been juggling as he waited for dawn. Finally! Now he could wake up his father. Milly had instructed him very firmly to let their father sleep in—at least until the sun was up.

"Dad, let's go!" Joe burst into the tent, pausing to shove his father's cowboy hat out of his face. He clambered onto his dad's cot and shook him. "The elephants need us."

Holt grumbled and rolled over, accidentally pushing Joe off the mattress.

Smiling, Joe stood and began juggling his apples once more.

"I think I heard one call out in the middle of the night, but I waited a while and it was quiet, so maybe I didn't, but now it's morning and they're all trumpeting at the sun, just like roosters. Maybe something's happening! Or maybe they're just saying they want breakfast."

Joe lost control of his apples and they rained down, mostly on his father.

From her cot, where she was braiding her hair, Milly smirked as Holt groaned.

"Good grief, Son," he mumbled. "Gonna make me miss the war."

But now that he was awake, Holt staggered to his feet, moving awkwardly to get ready. Milly and Joe waited outside. Milly wondered if he'd need help and almost went back in, but when Holt emerged, his left shirtsleeve was neatly tucked and pinned up out of the way.

He plucked his hat off Joe's head and strode off toward the elephants.

Rufus and his men had beaten them to the elephant cars and were already unloading the first two pachyderms, Goliath and Zeppelin. With his pole, Rufus banged on the ramp of Mrs. Jumbo's car.

"Move it, Mrs. Jumbo. Don't make me hafta incentivize you," he threatened.

All Joe could see was Mrs. Jumbo's back. She ignored Rufus, continuing to shove hay into a big pile. Was she making herself a bed?

His ears pink with annoyance, Rufus leapt up into the car and slammed his pole on the wall. The elephant turned, bellowing in concern.

"Easy, Rufus," Holt called out. "That's a lady in there."

Rufus sauntered to the doorway and sneered down at the Farrier family. "Oh, ho, look who's riding in to the rescue, but he ain't on the marquee no more. Time to see what he's been missing down here in the dirt. Ever git that feeling, Holt? Like there's something yer *missing*?"

"Imagine my surprise you didn't enlist," Holt parried back.

"Weak ticker," Rufus said, tapping his chest. "Doc's advice."

Joe seriously doubted that. Rufus was just not as brave and heroic as his dad. Nor did he understand serving the country, working for a greater cause. As far as Joe could tell, the only thing Rufus cared about was himself.

Rufus beckoned his men into the car and they

advanced on Mrs. Jumbo, who backed away nervously, trumpeting and swinging her head side to side.

"Dad, something's wrong. She doesn't want to leave," Milly said.

Reaching up, Rufus unhinged part of the wall and slammed it down, scaring Mrs. Jumbo. As she scrambled away, she wound up on the ramp, slipping and sliding toward the ground. The men hurried after her, herding her with their arms and poles. Rufus pushed on her head, shoving her backward down the ramp.

"Stop! She's scared!" Milly cried as the elephant rolled her eyes and stamped her feet.

Holt stormed forward. "All right, Rufus, leave her alone!"

He swung and punched the red-haired man, sending him sprawling.

Rufus spat at the ground. "Real chivalrous there, cowboy. Bet your dear departed would be proud."

"Dad, look!" Joe called from the top of the ramp.

Everyone spun to see him pointing at the pile of hay Mrs. Jumbo had been building. It was . . . moving.

Holt, Milly, and Joe edged toward it as Mrs. Jumbo trumpeted. Something within the pile stirred, and pieces of hay cascaded down, revealing two blinking dark eyes.

"Whoa," Holt said, a tremble of awe in his voice. "We got a baby in here."

\* \* \*

Down the train, in his personal car, Medici was lounging in a bath dictating to Rongo, who was balancing ledgers on his knees.

"Just look for cuts across the board," Medici said. "We're gonna advertise a sale, but raise prices ten percent. Are you getting all this?"

Rongo shot him a glare. "I'm the strongman." He wasn't supposed to be doing accounting *and* secretary work *and* inventory. He should be getting ready for his act.

"Baby! The baby's here!" someone called from outside.

"Baby? I'm a savant-garde genius!" Medici exclaimed, reaching for a towel and robe. "Get word to all the papers: 'The Medici Brothers Proudly Present . . . America's Newest Precious Bundle of Joy!'"

\* \* \*

Back in the elephant car, Holt was slowly shifting hay away from the newborn elephant, trying to coax it out of the pile.

"It's okay now. Don't be scared. Your mama's right outside." He was hoping the same soothing tone that worked on horses would transfer over.

A grayish pink circle with two nostrils poked out of the hay. The end of the trunk sniffed, then sneezed, spraying fluid right in Holt's face.

"Aah!" Holt backpedaled in surprise, bumping into Milly, who bumped into Joe, so they all tumbled down, thumping against the boxcar floor with a loud boom.

*"Eeeeeuuuugh!"* the baby elephant cried, scooting backward into the hay only to bang into the back of the car. This startled it even more, and it came zooming forward, shaking off hay in all directions.

Holt grabbed his kids and dove to the side as the elephant tripped and tumbled, end over end, down the ramp toward the gathering crowd of troupe members below.

"Oh, no!" called Miss Atlantis. Most people darted out of the way, but a few brave souls, Ivan among them, reached forward in concern.

"Where's my baby?" Medici called as he shoved to the front of the throng.

The ball of gray came to a stop, back legs splayed open. There was a flash of an adorable face, two beautiful shining black eyes, and a tiny trunk before—*flap*.

Two giant ears unfurled and landed over the animal's face, completely blocking it from view.

All the blood drained from Medici's face. "What. Is. That?"

"He's Baby Jumbo!" Joe said excitedly. But none of the adults shared his enthusiasm. They were all peering at the creature with dismay.

"But what are those?" Holt pointed at the gray flaps cloaking its face.

A trunk nudged out, parting the ears slightly. They billowed like curtains.

"That's not a baby; it's a blanket," Catherine said from her spot in the crowd. She crossed her arms, clearly disgruntled there wasn't a cute and cuddly creature to pet.

"It's a one-ton set of drapes," Ivan added.

"They do seem a little bit big," Milly offered.

Medici pulled on the sides of his hair, a gesture Holt recognized as panic. "I have fake freaks in the freak show. I don't need a real one in the center ring," the director yelled. "We've been swindled!"

Rufus clapped slowly, mocking Medici. "Congratulations, ya idiot. Gone and bought yourself a baby monster. Almost as clumsy as your kid, cowboy." He nodded at Holt and Joe before fixing his attention back on the elephant. "Hey, you think he can hear me?" He sprang toward it, shouting "Boo!"

The baby squeaked and shuffled back into the ramp. Mrs. Jumbo had had enough. She reached over the men holding her back and wrapped her trunk around Rufus's leg.

"Whoaa!" Rufus was suddenly hanging upside down off the ground. Then he flew through the air.

*Splash.* Rufus landed in a nearby water trough.

Laughter rang out among the troupe as he sputtered and scrambled out.

"Job's all yours, ya luckless lean-to," Rufus hissed at Holt as he stalked away. Rufus's two men followed him, releasing Mrs. Jumbo to move more freely.

The mother elephant hurried to her baby's side and gently nudged him up onto all fours. She patted him all over with her trunk—first, it seemed, to make sure he was unhurt, and then to tickle him affectionately. The baby nuzzled into her.

Some of the troupe members drifted away, but others remained to gawk at the spectacle. Medici spied Rongo, who'd just arrived from the office.

"Rongo, telegram to Brugelbecker: 'We've been

bilked with damaged goods. It's an aberration-travestation and I demand pecuniary recompense!' Do you have all that?"

The strongman gazed down at his notebook. "I have up to 'telegram.'"

"And whatever you do, don't call the papers. We can't advertise this baby." Medici paused and peered up at Rongo. "Tell me you didn't yet—did you?" His eyes grew wild.

Rongo stared back at him with a dumbfounded expression.

Medici pulled at his hair. "Aargh! Never do anything I tell you without checking with me first!"

Rolling his eyes, Rongo dropped the notebook and walked away.

Plonking down on a log, Medici scrubbed his head with his hands. "Why? Why me?" he moaned. "A face only a mother could love—"

"Sir, many of us find you handsome," Miss Atlantis said reassuringly.

Medici glared at her. "I was talking about the elephant."

"Look, she's drawing him a bath." Milly pointed to where Mrs. Jumbo was using her trunk to suck up water from the trough, then gently spraying it along the baby's back.

"Wait, that's it," Medici said, suddenly enthused. "A wash—whitewash, hogwash, brainwash. Holt!"

Holt stepped forward. "Need a vet to come look at him, Max?"

"What, a witness?" Medici shook his head. "We'll do no such thing. We're in Joplin for two whole weeks and we've promised them a beautiful baby. You have until tomorrow night to fix it."

The circus director stood and brushed off his pants as the cowboy blinked in astonishment.

"Me? This is my problem?"

"I'm the boss. I'm delegating," Medici proclaimed. "You tend to the elephants. Just make sure those ears disappear!"

Holt stared after him as Medici waltzed away. How was he going to just make somebody's ears disappear? He turned to the remaining performers, picking out Ivan from the group.

"Don't look at me!" The magician shook his head, hurrying off.

Water droplets landed on Holt's face as the baby elephant shook itself dry. Its ears were so large they dragged on the ground, immediately collecting dust.

Mrs. Jumbo trumpeted softly and wrapped her baby in a hug.

"Awww," Milly and Joe said together. They leaned against one another, their hearts warm.

But all Holt saw were those ears. Flapping, flopping ears. Ears five times the size of its head. Ears only a mother could love, indeed.

# RONGO
## JOPLIN, MISSOURI, 1919

y the light of an oil lamp, Rongo sat on his cot, holding a framed piece of paper. He stared at the photograph of himself at age nineteen, standing in a construction site. The caption underneath read RONGO JONES AND THE IMMENSE STEEL BEAM HE LIFTED TO SAVE THE LIVES OF 10 FELLOW WORKERS.

The reporters had circled for days, everyone wanting to know more about the day he'd held the heavy weight aloft as the foreman pulled each of the men trapped below it free.

"How'd you do it?" they asked.

"It was just something I had to do to get my crew out. I didn't think—I just picked it up," Rongo had replied. The truth was he'd always been a strong kid—hauling water for his parents on the farm, hefting bales of hay for neighbors during the summer and fall. He'd won every lifting competition with his friends, challenging each other to bigger and heavier objects. They'd always been in awe of him, cheering him on and slapping his back as *they walked home after one of their contests. Once con-struction had come in earnest to his part of Ohio, it had seemed like a natural fit for him.*

*After the rescue of his team, the town threw a parade for him, the families of the men welcomed him into their homes for dinner, and even the mayor met him—pinning a medal of valor on his coat.*

*Then the world moved on and everyone forgot about him. Sure, his crewmates still tipped their hats to him and wanted to work near him in case of another acci-dent, but in the streets he was once again invisible, just another man on his way to and from work.*

*Medici tracked him down and offered a life of fame and glory—promised him thousands of admiring fans everywhere he went and write-ups of all his tremendous feats. Rongo signed up on the spot, needing to feed that yearning in him to be seen.*

*Ha! Looking around his tent, Rongo wondered whether he'd tell his younger self to join up with Medici or not. At first it had been great, just what Medici promised—loads of awestruck people at each stop, not caring that he was a poor boy from Ohio, not caring that his skin was dark or that his teeth were crooked. All they cared about was his talents, like his strength. He'd heave up the barbells, twist and toss them in the air to catch them again and set them down gently, all with a practiced grimace.*

*Then he'd hurt his back, and Medici had downgraded him to fake barbells while he recuperated.*

*Rongo had never gone back to real weights.*

*Why not?*

*There'd been more to do, that was why. First Medici had asked him to help with camp setup when a few of their crew had run away; then it was "Can you be the drummer to lead into act announcements?" which morphed into becoming the one-man band. To make it bearable, Rongo wrapped his head in a towel to muffle the noise when he played—drums were much louder at only a foot's distance, he discovered.*

*Then, when Medici discovered Rongo's ability to track numbers (the strongman had beaten him at cards a few too many times), Rongo became the accounts manager and budget coordinator.*

You'd think that would mean a few housing perks, *Rongo thought bitterly, staring around his dilapidated tent. A rip in the ceiling meant he had to position his bed at an angle to avoid drips on rainy nights. Then again, nobody else was doing much better, so he shouldn't complain.*

*Yet nobody else had quite as many tasks piled on*

*them. It was as though Medici thought Rongo could carry the weight of the world, or at least the circus. He wished he could perfect his own strong act again. Maybe if he had time to focus on it, he could get back into shape and lift real weights overhead.*

*But it didn't seem there'd be time for that.*

*Even worse, Medici kept adding on new tasks and expectations. Now he was in charge of inventory? Rongo could keep track of boxes and crates, but live animals? That wasn't inventory. That was zookeeping.*

*And Medici wanted him to read his mind, too? He'd told him to send the telegram not five minutes before he'd gotten mad at him for doing so!*

*Rongo would ask for more pay, but he'd seen the ledgers—there was nothing to spare. He wouldn't leave, though. Not now. This was his home, his family. So, yeah, he'd tell his younger self that there'd be no better group of coworkers in the world—including Medici, most of the time.*

*"Hiya, Rongo," Puck called, tapping on his tent. "Can I come in?"*

*"Only if you can keep that monkey of yours contained from now on. I don't enjoy getting yelled at because he slipped out again," Rongo answered.*

*"I know, I know. I'll do my best."*

"Okay, come on in, Puck," Rongo said. He tucked the photo away on a shelf. No use dwelling on the past.

Puck shuffled in wearing his usual somber frown.

"What's the matter?" Rongo asked. "Miss Atlantis still won't look at you?"

Blushing, Puck nodded as he slumped onto an overturned crate that served as a chair. "All she sees is a lowly organ-grinder, churning out tunes for a monkey. She can't hear me from inside her tank, so how is she going to know I pour my heart and soul into the words? My talent is wasted!"

Rongo shook his head. "All you have to do is talk to her. If she knew you were interested, she might be, too. You never know."

"If only that were true." Puck sighed.

"Sometimes opportunity comes along, and sometimes you have to make your own opportunities, right?"

Rongo sat forward and pulled out a deck of cards.

Thwwwiiiit. He shuffled.

"Now, you going to mope all day or are you going to play?"

Puck perked up a little. "I'll play. But if I win, you have to listen to me rehearse my new Shakespearean bit."

Rongo grinned. "Then I better not lose, eh?"

# CHAPTER
# FIVE

arly the next morning, Joe tore across the circus grounds, Milly at his side. Ivan stopped them, asking if they'd had breakfast yet. It was sweet of Ivan to fret over them, but their dad was back now. Joe assured him they were fine and they scurried on their way to the elephant pens.

Mrs. Jumbo was in the ring practicing her act, so the little elephant was alone in a small enclosure. At the sight of them, he clambered to his feet and stumbled over to the fence, his ears trailing on the ground.

"Aww, look at him," Joe said. "Those giant ears just weigh him down."

"Hi, Baby Jumbo," Milly said, setting down a covered cage to wave to him. "Welcome to the circus. We're all family here, no matter how small."

She pulled back the blanket to reveal the miniature mouse circus cage. The three mice inside were already up and restless from the walk over.

"Umm, aren't elephants afraid of mice?" Joe asked.

"Says who?"

Her brother shot her a doubtful expression, and Milly continued. "That's why you experiment. Besides, someone needs to keep him company when he's not with his mom."

Behind the fence, the elephant's eyes—or what they could see of them behind his ears—widened as he watched the mice run through their act. The ringmaster, Timothy Q., scaled a small ladder to a platform and slid across a tightrope to another. Below him, the other mice ran on a wheel—one on the inside and one on top. Boldly, Timothy Q. leapt onto a net and then rolled to the ground, where he took a bow.

Milly dropped a peanut in for him as Joe clapped. The elephant let out a huff of air from his trunk, and the edge of his ear rose for a second.

"Look, he sees the peanuts." Joe pointed at the baby, an idea sparking. "Let's give him one if he can lift his ears out of the way!"

As Joe swung the peanuts back and forth in front of the elephant, the animal stopped puffing air and instead stretched his trunk as far as it could go between the rails, grasping for the food.

"No, you have to blow. Like this." Joe tried to demonstrate.

Milly laughed. "Good luck with that. Maybe you can teach him to juggle, too."

Joe frowned, elbowing his sister in the side. He wouldn't give up that easily. His dad was a superb animal trainer, and Joe had watched him for years. There must be something else he could try. He took off his dad's cowboy hat to scratch his head, and then he saw it—a small black feather in the hat's band.

"Aha!" Joe plucked the feather from the hat and placed it over his own eye. "Okay, look, Baby Jumbo." He blew air upward, lifting the feather to the side. "Now you try. You can do it—for the peanuts! Just do what I do. Blow!"

With a big puff, Joe sent the feather flying, and it drifted over the fence to land gently on Baby Jumbo's forehead.

*"Eeeeeuuugh!"* The elephant scrambled backward in alarm, then eyed the feather as it drifted down to the hay.

Slowly, his trunk inched out, sniffing at the strange item in his pen. He let out a tiny chuff and the feather danced into the air before settling on the ground again.

"No, not the feather. Your ears, blow to lift your ears," Joe coached.

But the elephant instead puffed out another burst of air toward the feather, launching it high in the air. It twirled back over the fence and landed at Joe's feet. The elephant almost seemed to smile at them.

Milly smiled back. "He thinks it's a game."

Always willing to play, Joe dropped to his stomach and blew the feather back through the fence. Baby Jumbo wriggled happily and mimicked Joe—legs splayed out to get his belly on the ground. He puffed, shooting the feather back to Joe.

"Hey, let me have a turn," Milly said. She plopped down next to her brother and sent the feather tumbling toward the elephant with a gentle exhale. As the baby puffed it back, Milly and Joe beamed at each other. They took turns guiding the feather back to the animal.

"Now stronger," Joe said. "With all your might." He sucked in a big breath and then whooshed it out to show the baby what he meant.

Baby Jumbo inhaled deeply, but to everyone's surprise, he accidentally sucked the feather toward him, and it shot up one of his nostrils. The elephant scrambled to his feet, hiccuping. His eyes and nose were twitching just like Milly's did when she dusted.

*"Ah-ah-ah-ah-chooooo!"* the elephant sneezed. With a whoosh, the feather cannoned out of his nose and his ears unfurled like butterfly wings.

Baby Jumbo rose into the air.

And stayed there.

Five feet off the ground.

His ears flapped, and then he tumbled to the ground in a pile.

Milly and Joe leapt to their feet, mouths open wide. Even the mice stared out from their cage, awestruck. The kids looked at each other to make sure they'd seen the same thing.

"Give him the peanuts," Joe said.

"You got it," Milly answered.

She flung the whole bag over the fence, and they took off without a word. Their dad had to hear this!

\* \* \*

Outside his family's tent, Holt was practicing with a rope lasso. He was lucky he was right-handed, he thought for the thousandth time since the war had claimed his other arm. Flicking his wrist, he sent the rope arcing through the air and noosed the toy he'd been aiming for.

"Yes!" Holt exclaimed, oblivious to the seething gaze fixed upon him.

Rufus lurked in the shadow of a nearby tent. He rubbed at his bandaged jaw and muttered. "Think you're still a big shot, huh? Got news for ya, cowboy. You're gonna be sorry you ever came back."

Rufus spotted the short figure of the circus director headed their way and slipped off.

"Max, come here, watch this," Holt shouted, waving Medici over. As soon as the circus owner was closer, Holt launched into his pitch. "Okay, forget the dozen horses. I figure all we need is one. I ride out and do some jumps." Holt mimed galloping out and leaping over barrels. "And then all of a sudden—a stampede!"

Holt kicked over a crate that had been blocking his tent flap, and a herd of poodles bounded out, yipping like crazy. The cowboy spun his lasso and flung it toward one, but the dog slipped through the hole and darted away to join the others.

"Still working out the timing," Holt said, turning back to Medici with a hopeful smile.

Medici's eyebrows quirked up. "Yeah," he said

indulgently, "it's coming along." His expression shifted as he tapped the long box at his side. "Meanwhile, for when you lead out the elephants, I had Costumes make you something." He offered up the box.

Swinging the rope over his shoulder, Holt flipped the box open. Inside lay a fake stuffed arm, complete with a flesh-toned hand with stubby fingers and a strap to attach it to his body.

"You really broke the bank with this one," Holt joked. It would fool people from a distance, but it looked like a scarecrow up close, lumpy and uneven. It was slightly longer than his real arm, meaning it would hang an inch or two lower.

"There are a lot of kids coming to the show . . ." Medici trailed off.

"So I don't scare anyone. I get it," Holt said with a nod. It would be bad for business if families stayed away on his account.

Just then, Joe's voice interrupted them. "Dad, it's Baby Jumbo! You have to come see!"

As his kids raced up, Holt jiggled the box so the top flipped closed. Joe tripped over the end of the rope and crashed into his father. The box crashed to the ground, spilling the arm out into the dirt.

Milly and Joe were too excited to notice, but Holt

ducked down and gathered it up as his children chattered at him.

"He jumped in the air . . . with his *ears*!" Milly exclaimed.

"It was amazing!" Joe added.

"Guys, I said leave him be." Holt's voice was gruff.

"But he was this far off the ground," Joe said, pointing above himself.

"Yeah, I'll bet he was," Holt drawled, rising to his feet, the box clutched to his chest. "He'll be tripping all over with ears like that."

"Dad, really. We tried an experiment," Milly began, but her father's cheeks were red as he spun around.

"This isn't a game! It's our livelihood. Stay out of his tent and leave the poor guy alone." Holt shoved the box inside the tent.

Milly stood back, arms crossed, assessing her father. If that was the way he was going to be, there was no point sharing the miracle they'd discovered with him. Her spine was stiff as she pivoted to Joe.

"First rule of science: you have to have interest. Otherwise, you don't deserve to know." Her dad had proved that he didn't even want to *try* to understand her, nor did he want to listen to them. Not even when what they had to tell him was the most incredible thing in the world. "Come on, Joe."

Holt grimaced as Milly stormed away, her brother trailing after her.

"Hard months on her, Holt," Medici said softly. "She's had to grow up way too fast."

"Annie knew how to talk to them." The cowboy slumped, deflated.

"Well. Can't fail until you start," Medici advised in a rare moment of wisdom. He patted Holt's shoulder and then headed off.

Holt watched his kids disappear around a tent corner, wishing he knew how to be a better dad, wishing his wife were still there, wishing things were different. But there was no wishing away his problems. It was time to tackle what he could—he had to figure out how to hide that elephant's ears before the performance that night.

# PRAMESH
## INDIAN EMPIRE, 1912

*The day of the contest had finally arrived. All the finest snake charmers in the Punjab region had been invited to compete, but* Pramesh's *brow was smooth. He knew his snakes, he'd practiced his moves, and his nephew,* Arav, *was the best assistant anyone could ask for.*

*The stones of the courtyard were cool now, but he knew the sun would beat down mercilessly upon them by the time the honorable judges arrived.*

Where to sit to avoid the sun? It appears I should have gotten up earlier, *Pramesh thought. Snakes were more sluggish when they were cool.*

*His rival,* Garjan, *grinned smugly from his chosen spot close to the arched walkway.*

Harrumph. No matter. He'll also be hard to pick out from the crowd.

*Waving to* Arav, *Pramesh marked out a four-foot ring in the southeast quadrant. He unrolled his mat and folded his legs under him, facing diagonally toward Garjan in order to keep an eye on his stiffest competition.*

*A throng of people had already gathered, surrounding the courtyard, craning to see the preparations. Arav and other assistants arranged their mentors' baskets around them.*

*"You fed them yesterday?" Pramesh asked unnecessarily—he'd watched his nephew do it.*

*"Yes, Uncle," Arav replied, ever polite, eager to learn the trade. As usual, he seemed afraid Pramesh would turn him away, despite the fact that Pramesh had always thought of him as the son he'd never had.*

*Nodding, Pramesh examined the woven baskets and inched one slightly to the right to give it more room from its neighbor.*

*They'd left their feistiest snake at home, as he required further training. There could be no mistakes today.*

*If all went well, he'd walk away with the prize—a paid trip across the ocean to America, where sponsors were eager to exhibit foreign acts for the benefit of wealthy, elite families.*

*"Should you rehearse? Test out their moods?" Arav asked.*

*"No, let's save it for the performance." Pramesh's snakes were more inclined to cooperate when they first*

*awakened. Warming them up would only make them quicker to lash out.*

*Around midday, the judges arrived—the local magistrate, with the British deputy commissioner in his wake. The latter looked mildly ill, but maybe that was just his milky-white skin. His attendants carried a covering for him so he wouldn't have to stand directly in the sun. The magistrate and deputy commissioner paused to survey the courtyard full of snake charmers.*

*At last! Pramesh's back straightened and he adjusted his turban. Taking a meditative breath, he closed his eyes and envisioned his performance—how he'd pick up his pungi, play a few notes, then open up the first basket and free the snake.*

*But apparently Pramesh would have to wait a bit longer. The deputy commissioner and his entourage wound their way through, letting one snake charmer perform at a time.*

*Arav crouched next to his uncle and watched as Pramesh offered commentary on each.*

*"Kuldip is too aggressive and impatient with his snakes—see how he prods them out with his foot? It is best to tap near the basket so the snake senses the vibration. If you poke the serpent, it will rear up and might lash out.*

*"Ah, what is Jasveer thinking? That is a spitting*

cobra," Pramesh muttered as they watched the charmer next to them.

Sure enough, the angry snake angled its head and sent a spray of venom toward the young man. Jasveer was able to shield his eyes, but in the chaos, the cobra began to flee, whipping its body toward the deputy commissioner himself.

"Eeeek!" the deputy commissioner squeaked, backpedaling into his attendants.

Seizing his chance, Pramesh vaulted over his baskets, landing lightly on his feet, and grabbed the snake behind its head.

The cobra writhed but couldn't spray due to Pramesh's firm grip. Instead, it wound its tail along his arm. Calmly, Pramesh nodded to the deputy commissioner, whose eyes were wide with fear and relief, his skin even paler than before. Then Pramesh skillfully returned the cobra to Jasveer's basket, where Arav waited with the lid to shut it in again. Jasveer hung his head in shame and began packing up his baskets. He knew he was out.

Once the snake was contained, Pramesh bowed with his hands pressed together to the deputy commissioner, whose shoulders relaxed.

"Thank you," the deputy commissioner said. "What is your name?"

"I am Pramesh, honorable sir."

*"Well, Pramesh, you handle snakes expertly. I am grateful to you. Let us see what else you can do." The deputy commissioner gestured for him to sit.*

*Pramesh folded himself into his spot. Gently, he picked up each of his three baskets, one by one, and breathed a puff of air into them lightly. This let his snakes know it was time and that he was there. Next he picked up his pungi, blew a few notes, and gently uncovered the first basket.*

*Sadhana, his favorite serpent, unwound herself from her rest and raised her top third, eyeing him warily. Her tongue flicked, and as Pramesh wove the pungi back and forth, she flared her hood, displaying the beautiful marking on the back of her head for the deputy commissioner. Of course, Sadhana didn't mean to be beautiful. She was trying to intimidate the pungi (and Pramesh) into leaving her alone. Her head followed the movements of the instrument, considering it a threat.*

*Once she was steady in position, Pramesh unboxed the second snake. Nadin was sluggish at first, but when Pramesh tapped the ground with his foot, the snake rose up and flared his hood as well. Pramesh played and swayed gently, guiding his snakes back and forth. Then he carefully used the lids to cover first Sadhana and then Nadin. When they were both back to resting, he set them to the side and moved the third box closer.*

*"And now, honorable sir, allow me to introduce you to something you may have never seen!" Pramesh said.*

*Arav removed the cover and Pramesh extended his hand into the basket itself, gently tugging on the snake within.*

*The deputy commissioner gasped as Pramesh pulled out a yellow-and-white snake. The serpent kept coming, winding itself up Pramesh's arm, pausing to flick its tongue in his ear, then continuing behind his neck and down his other arm, coming to rest its head on his other hand. It had to be over five feet long.*

*"What is it?" the British man asked.*

*"An* ajgar, *Your Grace. A python," Pramesh answered. The man was unlikely to know that this species strangled its prey and had no venom. Even if he did, Pramesh was confident Tanak was an impressive creature. "One with a most unusual pigmentation."*

*"Quite extraordinary. Extraordinary indeed."*

*As the deputy commissioner moved away with the magistrate, Pramesh caught Garjan's eye and smirked. From the glower Garjan wore, he didn't have anything better stowed away in his pots. Indeed, the deputy commissioner moved through the rest of the performers quickly, and while Garjan put on a good show, he had nothing out of the ordinary in his repertoire.*

*Pramesh beamed as the deputy commissioner announced him as the winner.*

*He'd done it!*

I'm going to America! *he thought.*

*Bowing and thanking the deputy commissioner, Pramesh couldn't wait for his journey to start. He'd heard they didn't have jungles in America, so he'd need to bring everything his snakes would require to keep them healthy—there'd be no heading out into the wilderness to find replacements. But surely they had rats there for his snakes to eat.*

*Pramesh's brother and sister-in-law jumped up and down, giddy with excitement when he found them in the crowd. Then his brother's face grew serious.*

*"You will take Arav with you, won't you? He would love to go."*

*"But won't you need him here, to help with the farm?"*

*Pramesh's brother and his wife exchanged a look. "We discussed it, and we want Arav to travel, to see the world with you and continue to learn the trade. His future is brightest with you."*

*Pramesh turned to regard Arav. The boy was strong and promising, and Pramesh would certainly enjoy having family by his side. "Do you really want to come?" Pramesh asked him. He would not force someone into* an arrangement they did not embrace. That would be a recipe for regret and ruin.

Solemnly, Arav nodded. "It would be my great honor to accompany you, Uncle."

"Then it is settled. Arav will come with me."

Pramesh smiled as his family celebrated. In a week's time, he and Arav would be on their way across the rolling seas to the waving hills of grain and grass and bustling cities of America, a land where newcomers could find opportunity and where, apparently, they were so curious about snake charmers that they were willing to grant the best of the best a paid trip to demonstrate the art.

I'm the best of the best! Pramesh thought gleefully as he carried his snakes home to his hut. In the streets, people waved and bowed and children rushed over to brush against his arm in the hopes his wisdom and experience would transfer to them.

If this was the way his own villagers behaved after his win, imagine what Americans who had never seen a snake charmer before would do! Pramesh vowed to represent his people with strength and grace. He'd show America the powerful traditions of snake charming without any of the terrible tricks today's charlatans used—like sewing up a snake's mouth or defanging it and removing its venom sacs.

*Imagine harming a living creature so! No, Pramesh was the best of the best and he needed no such shortcuts. He knew snakes and their beauty. Now to share them with America!*

# CHAPTER
## SIX

oplin's citizens crowded through the gate as soon as the circus opened that night, eager to finally see inside. Barely anybody noticed the bucket with a roughly painted sign reading MEDICI HORSE FUND. ONE HORSE ONLY. DONATIONS WELCOME! And anybody who *did* see it didn't drop any money in—they were saving it for the food and wonders within the circus.

Along each side of the pathway booths were set up with magnificent posters unfurled behind the stages for each performer in the show—from a gentleman juggler to tightrope walkers.

Joplin's citizens crowded in front of a tank holding

a genuine mermaid! People gawked at her emerald tail and craned their heads to look for gills. Miss Atlantis twisted and kept her movements fluid, so it would seem as though she was moving through the water that was actually trapped in the double-paned glass of the tank.

"Look at that!" someone cried, pointing at the next booth.

A miniature stage had been set up and standing on it was a real live monkey holding up a tiny skull. From the side, his back to the crowd, Puck squeezed the concertina and recited the lines for Barrymore.

"'To be or not to be, that is the question!'" Puck exclaimed. Before he could continue, Barrymore tossed the skull away and plunked a blond wig on his head. Puck switched over to *Romeo and Juliet*, doubting that anybody in the audience would recognize it. But at least a monkey in a wig got some laughs.

Opposite him, the Rubberband Man was twisted, his head between his legs. The next booth over was the strongman's.

Rongo hefted the fake barbells over his head, grimacing in pretend exertion. Only a handful of people clapped. The Joplin crowd was lackluster.

"Rongo, let's go," Medici hissed from behind a banner.

Sighing, the strongman dropped the weights and followed Medici to the Big Top, where the main show was about to start. There were still some ticket buyers taking in the performers, though, including a crowd around the snake charmer.

Pramesh sat cross-legged on a pillow, playing his pungi, gently coaxing one of his snakes up from its woven basket just a few feet away. Arav hovered nearby in case he was needed.

In his audience, a group of teenaged boys jostled to the front.

"That ain't no snake," one of them shouted, convinced it was all a trick. "It's just a ding-a-ling on a wire. Heck, I could do it."

Pramesh calmly stopped the music and faced the impertinent youth. "As you wish," he said, inclining his head.

With his foot, he tipped over the basket, setting free his smallest cobra. The snake hissed and slithered across the small stage away from Pramesh—and toward the crowd.

"Uncle!" Arav raced to scoop it up as the crowd shrieked and fled in all directions.

Pramesh sniffed. "When I was young, we believed."

Luckily, a drumroll from the main tent signaled the start of the big show, and most people headed toward it. Arav seized the cobra behind its head and eased it into the basket, firmly shutting the lid on it again.

"Uncle, please." His eyes implored the older man.

"Okay, fine, I'll behave," Pramesh muttered. "But in India we raise our children to respect their elders. And we know there is more to the world than what the eye can see. Americans are too quick to doubt."

"Yes, Uncle," Arav said. "Much in America is not what we expected."

Pramesh harrumphed as he watched the circus attendees file into the main tent.

\* \* \*

Inside the Big Top, Joplin's citizens settled onto the tiered seats and gazed at the empty ring. Two curtains hid corners of the tent, and a slit in the back served as the entrance for the performers.

From the far end of the bleachers, Rongo tapped grumpily on a xylophone, then switched a stick for the beat-up trumpet and blasted out a few toots. The cymbals were next; he stomped on a pedal to knock a drum at the same time.

From his place backstage, Medici shot Rongo a look, wishing the man would play with a bit more enthusiasm. The music sounded different when Rongo was in a good mood. Shrugging, Medici squared his shoulders, smoothed down his red coat, and strode out into the spotlight.

"Welcome, Joplin, Missouri! Ladies and gentlemen, boys and girls," he boomed out, from the center of it all—the ring. It was a smaller crowd than he'd have liked. Where were all the people? Didn't anyone come to the circus anymore? "I am your master of ceremonies, the one, the only . . . Maximillian Medici!" He paused, but nobody clapped, so he quickly went on. "And now I give you the artistry of the Medici Brothers' Circus!"

He swung his arm wide to signal the rest of the troupe.

Clowns in animal costumes, Ivan and Catherine, and the acrobats burst into the ring from the back flap, cartwheeling and throwing confetti. There was a smattering of applause in the crowd. Medici hid a grimace as he ducked off to change his costume. These folks were hard to please.

* * *

Backstage, Holt scratched at the straps holding the fake arm onto his shoulder. He stooped down to make sure the little elephant's ears were tied up well with the big blue bow the costume crew had given him. The little guy squirmed a bit. Holt felt a pang. *I know how you feel,* he thought.

Aloud, he said, "Okay, little guy, let's put on a show." Holt turned away to make sure the other elephants were set. Mrs. Jumbo, who would not be going out until after the trapeze act, reached forward and caressed her baby, who was drinking in all the sounds from the ring.

Onstage, the clowns pretended to wobble as they carried out a large box labeled DYNAMITE! HANDLE WITH CARE! and set it down center-ring. With a boom, the box's sides flew open and a cloud of smoke filled the air.

Medici stepped through it with a flourish, only now he was decked out in a blue jacket, wore a black wig, and had pasted on bushy eyebrows and a mustache. When he spoke, he coated his words in a thick pretend Italian accent. "Friends, I am Giuseppe Medici. My brother and I are honored tonight to introduce to you, making his worldwide debut, first-ever baby elephant born right here in America! Please welcome the pride of this circus, our dear Baby Jumbo!"

Rongo squeezed the accordion under one arm while blowing into the trumpet (which was propped up on a stand), banging the drum with his foot and clanging the cymbals together.

Right on cue, Holt led Goliath and Zeppelin into

the ring. Banners of storks draped their sides, and two acrobats perched on top of them, holding blankets bundled to look like babies. Holt eased the elephants into a walk around the ring, keeping the fake arm on the side away from the audience. Not five steps in, he heard a man call out.

"Isn't that Holt Farrier? The Stallion Star? Ain't you Holt Farrier?"

Holt ducked his head, gritting his teeth. "He died in the war," Holt said flatly.

As Zeppelin lumbered forward, the rope tied to his tail tugged a blue bassinet into view. The crowd let out a collective "aww" as they caught sight of the baby elephant inside, a giant pacifier gripped in his mouth. Baby Jumbo swayed on his feet, eyes wide at the lights and colors and people all around. Inching forward, the parade passed a beautiful pink-feathered hat. Baby Jumbo perked up.

Dropping the pacifier, he turned his head to track the hat as the performers went around the ring for a second time. As the bassinet drew closer, he leaned against the side, reaching his trunk through. But he missed the hat.

"What's he doing?" Milly asked from behind the curtain.

Joe peered out as well. "Saying hi to the lady."

"No. It's her hat! He's reaching for the feathers." Milly shot Joe a horrified look. "He thinks that gets him peanuts."

Milly ducked into the tent and crept forward, trying to stay low. "Dad," she whisper-called. "Keep him back from the side—"

But Holt didn't hear her. The elephants circled again, and this time the baby leaned as close to the audience as he could and sucked the feathers up. Unfortunately, the hat came with them . . . as did the blond wig of the woman who'd been wearing it.

"Aaaah!!!" The woman shrieked as others in the audience laughed. The woman's husband rose with a roar, pointing at the offending elephant.

Medici, in the midst of a backstage costume swap, froze as he spotted the baby. His nose—plugged with feathers—was twitching uncontrollably.

*"Ah-ah-ah—"*

"Oh, please, I beg of you, no!" Medici cried.

*"Chooooo!!!!"*

Blown backward by the force of his sneeze, Baby Jumbo flew out of the bassinet, losing his diaper and bow in the process. He landed on his bottom in the center of the ring, his ears slowly floating down to join him like two giant quilts. Everyone froze, stunned into silence for a moment.

*"Ah-choo."* Baby Jumbo snorted out two last feathers.

Zeppelin and Goliath were the first to react. Shying backward, they trumpeted in alarm.

"Whoa, easy now," Holt called, reaching out to steady them. "He's an elephant, same as you."

"That ain't a real elephant," someone in the crowd called. "Those ears are fake!"

"What did you do to that thing?" someone else cried.

Medici burst out from backstage. "Why, Missouri, this is astonishing. A rare curiological oddity. Giuseppe, where are you? Come see!" He spun in a circle, pretending to look for his brother and gesturing at his troupe to do something—anything!

The crowd erupted in boos and hisses. Baby Jumbo spotted Milly and Joe. He blew his ears up and onto his back. His trunk poked at one of the feathers that was now drifting through the air, and he puffed it toward Goliath, trying to start a game.

The other elephants reared up, sending the performers on top of them tumbling down to the ground. Holt sprang forward to grab hold of Zeppelin's trunk.

"Look, the other ones are scared of it, that's how you know it's fake," another heckler called.

"No, no, he's real! He's just a freak," Medici cried.

He leaned toward Holt and hissed, "Get those ears off the stage."

Baby Jumbo flopped forward, eager to get closer to fellow elephants, but somersaulted over his ears. People started laughing. Then someone noticed the sign over the bassinet had been rearranged in the chaos. The D from DEAR BABY JUMBO had fallen off to hook over the J; the sign now read EAR BABY DUMBO.

"Dum-bo! Dum-bo!" the crowd chanted and hollered, hurling food at the ring. Hot dogs and popcorn rained down on the baby, who used his ears to shield himself.

Backstage, Mrs. Jumbo paced anxiously. Rufus stalked up, whip in hand. He sneered at her, smiling maliciously and cracking the whip at her feet. "Hear 'em making fun of your ugly baby? Who is gonna help him now?"

*"EEEEAAAUUUGGGGHHH!!!!"* Mrs. Jumbo trumpeted loudly. She fled into the main ring.

Rufus followed her in, his face plastered with fake fear. "Stop her! The beast's gone mad!" he yelled. Then he slyly cracked the whip again before ducking under the seats to watch the spectacle.

Performers scattered as Mrs. Jumbo rumbled through the tent, head swinging back and forth in alarm, ears flapping wildly. Spotting her baby just as a bucket of popcorn hit him in the face, she charged toward him, quickly placing herself between him and the stands in a protective stance. The ground shook as she raised her front feet and brought them down with a boom.

Screams filled the tent; the audience stampeded for the exits.

"Everyone out," Medici cried. "Get to safety."

Milly and Joe dove under the tiered benches to avoid getting trampled by the mob as Ivan, Catherine, Rongo, and the clowns helped guide people out. Onstage, the baby elephant hid behind his mother, whose ears were flared in anger.

Pramesh rushed into the tent to help Holt guide Goliath and Zeppelin away from the madness. Once Pramesh had the male elephants outside, Holt raced back inside to soothe Mrs. Jumbo.

He eased closer, hand out low. "No one's going to hurt your baby. We're here to protect him, just like you."

Mrs. Jumbo huffed, swinging her trunk. But she stopped trumpeting and peered at Holt's outstretched hand.

*Crack!* From underneath the benches, Rufus cracked his whip again.

Startled, Mrs. Jumbo backpedaled into one of the

tent's support poles. Her weight crashed into it, splintering it in two. She darted to the side, ushering her baby with her, as the top half of the pole broke off and plummeted down toward the benches.

"Milly, Joe, watch out!" Holt yelled as he ran toward them.

Scrambling, he pulled them out just as the pole crashed into the seats. Rufus was not as lucky; the benches crushed him to the ground.

Billows of red-and-white-striped fabric surrounded the Farriers as they struggled free of the tent.

After a few long moments, the dust settled and the circus quieted.

Outside, the Joplin crowd had fled, but the troupe stood in a circle, faces somber. Now that the chaos was over, Mrs. Jumbo was gently nuzzling her baby, patting him all over to make sure he was okay. Holt and Pramesh herded the rest of the elephants back to their pens and locked them in. Then, at Medici's direction, they quarantined Mrs. Jumbo in an old lion's cage. Her baby circled around the outside, poking his trunk through the bars to reach his mother.

"What happens now?" Joe asked Holt once he returned.

"Don't worry, we'll be fine," Holt said, pulling his kids in for a hug.

Milly stepped away, her eyes on another family. "He means to Mrs. Jumbo."

The mother elephant was pressed against the bars, her trunk wrapping her baby's ears around him to keep him warm. She tucked him against the cage, as close as she could get to him. The baby elephant looked up at her happily, but his mother's eyes were troubled.

Milly's father had no answer. In the distance, police sirens wailed, en route to the circus. Several men carried Rufus's lifeless form out on a stretcher.

A grim Medici moved among his troupe, making sure everyone else was safe, before going to greet the police. It would be a long and difficult night.

# CHAPTER
## SEVEN

he next morning, a large truck hauling a massive cage on a flatbed pulled up to the circus. H. M. BRUGELBECKER—ANIMAL PURVEYORS. BILOXI, EST. 1874 read the sign on the side of the truck.

A tall bushy-haired man exited the truck's cab and gazed around the circus. He wore a light cotton suit that was completely out of place in the field. After studying the collapsed tent, he stalked up the steps of the caboose and barged inside.

Medici leapt out of his desk chair.

"You promised me a mother and a beautiful baby.

Not a freak-bearing beast that would ruin my show," Medici cried, wringing his hands together.

Brugelbecker shrugged. "Did I train her? Was I here? She was not provoked on my account."

"I have a man dead, do you understand?" Medici pulled at what was left of his hair. He yanked a newspaper from his desk and thrust it into Brugelbecker's face so he could read the headline: KILLER BEAST ON THE RAMPAGE! DEADLY MEDICI CIRCUS STRIKES MISSOURI.

Brugelbecker casually moved the paper aside. "A deal is a deal. You have no legal claim."

"Brugelbecker, I'm a man of ethics."

The taller man raised his eyebrow as though he doubted that.

Medici drew himself up to his full unimpressive height. "You have a moral responsibility to buy your killer elephant back."

"And what of the baby?" Brugelbecker asked.

"At least he got a few laughs," Medici said. "I'll put him in the clown act to try and salvage something."

Brugelbecker's eyes narrowed and he chewed on his lip as he weighed the options.

"I'll buy her back at half price," he finally said.

"Full price," Medici insisted.

"Quarter price."

"Half price it is!" Medici stuck out his hand and

106

the two men shook on it. At least Medici would be rid of the dangerous creature. He hoped the bad press would die down soon.

* * *

Brugelbecker and his crew backed their truck up as close to Mrs. Jumbo's cage as possible. Mrs. Jumbo let out an uneasy cry at the commotion. One of the men unlocked her cage and the others began herding her out, prodding her with sticks to make her move faster when she stopped.

Bellowing, Mrs. Jumbo swung her head to find her baby, who was happily trying to tackle her tail.

Milly and Joe rushed over at the noise. They found their father, Pramesh, and Medici amid the small crowd of performers watching the strangers try to coax Mrs. Jumbo onto a ramp attached to the truck.

"What's happening?" Milly asked frantically. "Where are they taking her?"

"Get away." Holt shooed them off. "Go back to your tent."

Brugelbecker's men shoved at Mrs. Jumbo's rear, but she was immovable. The baby trotted around the base of the ramp, trying to poke through the crowd to his mother's side.

Milly fumed. It hadn't been Mrs. Jumbo's fault the

tent collapsed on Rufus—it was an accident! Now she was being carted away like she was dangerous when all she'd done was try to protect her baby—as any mother would.

"But she's his *mother*!" Joe cried. They couldn't do this. It was wrong to separate a mother and her baby. Wrong!

"Dad, please. Stop them. Please!" Milly pleaded.

With an expert tap on the rump, Brugelbecker got Mrs. Jumbo moving again. The ramp rumbled as she thundered up it and into the waiting cage. Brugelbecker slammed the door shut and locked it. The elephant pivoted in the small space to find her son. He was trundling up the ramp toward her, tripping on his ears.

Several circus crew members jumped in, grabbing hold of the baby just short of his mother. His feet scrambled on the ramp and he extended his trunk as far as he could, straining to reach her. Mrs. Jumbo stretched out to him as well, only inches between them.

Tears collected in Joe's eyes as he turned to his father. "Do something. *Do* something."

"Mama would have done something," Milly said.

Holt's shoulders slumped. "Mom's not here." Resigned, he joined the crew at the ramp and looped a rope over the baby elephant's leg. "I know, little friend, I do," he whispered soothingly.

With the rope over his shoulder and the other men pitching in, they tugged the elephant down the ramp. The little elephant called out in alarm, his mother answering back, equally worried.

Milly put her arm around Joe. None of this was fair. The world was hard enough; why would they take someone's mother away like this? The gathered crowd of performers knew it was wrong. Rongo was holding back tears, Catherine held tightly to Ivan, and Miss Atlantis was openly sobbing. Pramesh stepped up to the cage and placed his forehead against the bars.

"Beautiful creature," he said. "We'll take care of your son."

*Clank.* Brugelbecker's team slid the ramp up under the flatbed and climbed into the truck.

"*Viel Glück*, Max Medici," Brugelbecker called. "Tell your 'brother' I said *auf Wiedersehen*."

Joe broke away, running for the tents, Milly just steps behind him. Still at the baby elephant's side, Holt saw them leave with another stab of regret. But he had to do his job. The truck churned off, sending dust flying. Long after it was out of sight, everyone could hear Mrs. Jumbo crying out and her son answering pitifully.

# CHAPTER
# EIGHT

 ripping sound woke Milly in the middle of the night. Sitting up, she found her father perched on a crate. He was ripping up papers by trapping one end under his boot and then yanking back with his good hand on the other side. Everything went into the trash bin.

Bleary eyes found hers. "Darling, it's late."

Dumping the last scraps into the bin, he staggered out of the tent and into the night. Curious, Milly moved over to investigate the bin. Inside she found her dad's new fake arm and a stack of Stallion Stars publicity shots. Her father had torn them right down the center, splitting himself off from their mother. Milly reached in to rescue a few of her favorites and tucked the pieces into her trunk. Her father might want them back later.

She wrapped a jacket around her shoulders and checked on Joe, but he appeared to be asleep, so she ducked out of the tent. She knew someone else who was probably having trouble sleeping and might like some company.

The baby elephant lay on the hay, looking like a popped balloon. He didn't lift his head or even twitch as Milly slipped inside the boxcar with him, but his eyes were open, gazing at the wall. In the corner, the mice squeaked a welcome. Milly sank to the floor and petted the elephant's head.

His eyes rolled back toward her before sliding away.

"I know. I can't sleep, either," she said. She fingered the key she wore around her neck. "My mama told me there'd be times when my life seemed locked behind a door. So she gave me this key that her mama gave her. She said whenever I have that feeling, imagine that door and just turn the key."

The elephant peered at her as though asking, *Does it work?*

Milly shrugged. "I keep trying."

Picking up one of his soft ears, she stroked the outside, smoothing it across her lap. When she paused, he flicked it at her, so she smiled and kept patting.

"You're not supposed to be in here alone," someone said.

Joe stood in the boxcar door, his pillow in hand, but it was a lot lumpier than usual.

"I'm not alone now. You're here," she said. "What's that?"

"I just thought he might be hungry," Joe said as he joined her. He opened the pillowcase, showing her the mound of peanuts inside.

Milly shook her head. "He's sad. You don't eat when you're sad."

"The mermaid does," Joe countered. He knelt down next to Milly and sprinkled some peanuts in front of the elephant, but the baby didn't even sniff them.

"Come on. Have one, Dumbo." Joe nudged a few closer, so they were almost touching his trunk.

"We're calling him Dumbo now?" Milly wasn't sure she liked it.

"If we call him Baby Jumbo, it might make him miss his mom," her brother explained.

Milly picked up a peanut, turning it over. "Here you go, Junior." She waved it in front of his trunk. "Little Guy. Big Ears."

"C'mon, just say it."

"Here you go, Dumbo," Milly said, giving in. "Flap those ears again, to show us we didn't imagine it."

Dumbo refused to move.

Milly dropped the peanut and Joe scooped the handful of them off the floor and stashed them in his pillowcase again.

"She didn't mean to hurt anyone," Joe said, scratching Dumbo's back. "She was just protecting you. And *we* think your ears are great."

When Dumbo still didn't respond, Joe's shoulders slumped. "Maybe he wants to be alone. Like Dad."

"Nobody wants to be alone," Milly sighed, getting to her feet.

Joe stood up, too, then poured the peanuts into a big pile on the floor.

"Well, if you change your mind . . . Night-night, Dumbo," he said.

Joe tucked his pillow under his arm, and he and Milly turned to leave the boxcar. A few feathers drifted out of the pillow as they walked away, then a few more. Dumbo's eyes caught on them and his trunk crept toward them. He lurched after the kids, trunk-first, vacuuming up the trail of feathers falling in their wake.

"*Ah-ah-ah-achooo!*" Dumbo sneezed.

Milly and Joe whirled and saw Dumbo hovering behind them, ears flapping, a small smile on his face. Milly's eyes nearly fell out of her head and Joe's jaw dropped.

Another feather slipped out of the case and Dumbo zeroed in on it, shooting toward it with a cute little spin of his tail. He caught the feather, but was so excited he didn't pay attention to where he was going and bumped into the wall, landing in a pile of hay.

"Did you see that?" Milly shrieked.

"Did you see that?" Joe asked at the same time.

"I asked you first," they blurted together. Milly wheeled her arm to point at Dumbo, sending another feather up into the air.

The elephant leapt forward, ears flapping and trunk out to—*swooopft*—suck up the feather. His ears flared out in an attempt to slow down, but he crashed into the ceiling anyway, and then careened toward the far wall. Wrapping his ears around himself, he bounced off the wall like a ball and rolled along the floor . . . straight toward the kids.

Milly and Joe dove to the side just in time. With a thump, Dumbo hit the wall where he'd started, this time in an upside-down ball. He wriggled right-side up and peered out at them apologetically.

"It's not the peanuts that made him do it—it's the

feathers!" Milly ripped a handful from the pillow's lining and flung them in the air.

Dumbo's tail twirled and he flew up to catch them, but this time he used his ears to steady his flight and managed to steer clear of the walls, circling back to them with three feathers gripped in his trunk. His eyes twinkled and his mouth was open in a wide grin.

"He's having fun!" Joe clapped.

In their cage, the mouse performers chirped and bounced up and down like they were cheering as Dumbo sailed to a perfect stop, four feet flat on the ground.

Joe raced to one side of the car, scooping up feathers just as his sister ran to the other. They began calling Dumbo back and forth, tossing feathers as high as they could. Dumbo soared into the air, flapping madly to try to collect them all.

"It's his ears. He can fly," Milly said in awe.

"Kwaaa-chooo!" Dumbo let out a massive sneeze, shooting himself backward. Out of control, he crashed near the mouse cage, and its door popped open. The mice skittered out and darted away, afraid of being trampled. Dumbo lifted Timothy Q. with his trunk to peer at him.

"Eeek!" Timothy Q. squeaked, not wanting to find himself flying through the air. He jumped off Dumbo's nose and buried himself in the nearest haystack.

As Joe gathered up more feathers, Milly stared at the baby elephant. "Dumbo, you gotta do this in the show," she said.

"What do you mean?" Joe asked.

Milly turned to him, excitement flushing her cheeks. "Because if the circus sells more tickets and Medici makes more money . . . then we could get him to use some to buy Mrs. Jumbo back!"

"Yes!" Joe pumped his fist in the air. "Milly, you are so smart. You *will* be a scientist someday."

Milly rubbed Dumbo's forehead, pressing her own to his. "We can get her back, Dumbo. *You* can. You just show them all what you can do."

Dumbo leaned into her trustingly.

"C'mon, we gotta tell Dad!" Joe beelined for the door.

Milly spun and blocked him, their last conversation with Holt about Dumbo fresh in her mind. "No. He'll just tell us to be practical." She paced the floor. "Shows got cancelled for a week, right?" Joe nodded. "We can research and study and test."

Exhausted, Dumbo flopped to the floor and began shoveling peanuts into his mouth. The kids beamed down at him.

"You're a miracle elephant, Dumbo," Milly said. "And we're going to bring your mama home."

# CHAPTER
# NINE

 week later, the circus reopened. Medici had sent performers all throughout Joplin to talk up the newest act and reassure everyone of the beefed-up security measures. A small crowd had shown up and Medici was frantic—running around to make sure nothing went wrong. If tonight's audience had a good time, ticket sales might triple tomorrow.

Milly and Joe flanked Dumbo backstage, patting him soothingly as they fitted a yellow rain jacket and black fireman's hat onto him. Onstage, the clowns were in the midst of their firefighting act, complete with an oversized ladder. The oldest clown, Spiros,

117

swung around on it, toppling his comrades to the audience's delight. Up above, a platform shaped like a house was ablaze with real flames. Barrymore squeaked dramatically from one of its windows. Below him, a pool of water served as a landing spot, as well as a draw for the clown firemen's hoses.

It was all carefully staged; both the clowns and Barrymore were perfectly safe. Even so, Milly and Joe's stomachs churned. Soon Dumbo would be out there, too. They hadn't had time to practice the act with the fire. What if he panicked and charged the crowd? Would Medici send him away, too?

Joe slung a protective arm over the baby elephant while Milly gave him a quick pep talk.

* * *

Unaware of the kids' plan, Holt peered out at the small audience and fiddled with his costume.

"This is an all-time low," he muttered, adjusting the oversized fireman's jacket and the blindingly bright helmet for the hundredth time.

Coming to join him, Medici laughed. "Who said he didn't want to be recognized? You!" He passed the kids and squatted down in front of Dumbo. "Okay, Big D, just like in rehearsal . . . except with lights, music, fire, and crowds."

Milly scratched Dumbo's ear. "For your mama," she whispered.

"Please, God, let them laugh at an elephant clown," Medici prayed as Holt nudged Dumbo out behind the curtain.

Lights blinded the little elephant. Noise filled his ears—the cacophony of unfamiliar sounds a deafening roar to his sensitive hearing. Shuffling forward, he stepped on his ear and tumbled to the ground, crashing into a man in front of him.

Laughter filled the tent. Medici nearly wept with relief. But he didn't let up his grip on his top hat.

Spiros, the clown he'd knocked over, sprang up and whirled on Dumbo, fist raised in mock fury. Dumbo cowered back. His head swung side to side as though looking for someone to guide him.

"Show 'em, Dumbo," Holt heard Milly say. "You can do it! Show 'em all like you showed us!"

Holt frowned. What was she talking about? Shaking his head, he let out a sharp, low whistle.

Dumbo perked up at his cue. Animals liked to know what was expected of them. Dumbo was no different. He trundled over to the pool and sucked up water with his trunk. Several clowns pointed up at the platform above. Dumbo aimed. Holt whistled twice. Dumbo swung on command and—

*Sploooosh!*

The water spray hit the clowns right in their faces, knocking them down. Again, the audience hooted in delight. Dumbo filled his trunk from the pool just as the clowns staggered to their feet. Frantic, they shook their fingers "no" at him and pointed again to the burning platform. At Holt's whistle—*splooosh!*—the firemen were blasted to the floor.

"They love it!" Medici cheered as the audience clapped.

Onstage, they had moved to the next sequence. A "ladder" ramp was raised and attached to the platform. Following his cues, Dumbo siphoned up water once more, but this time, the clowns and Holt prodded him up the ramp toward the platform. A loud noise from the crowd made Dumbo jump. His eyes darted around the tent, landing on a group of boys flapping their hands like they were ears, mocking him. He sank back, his tail tucked down.

"He won't fly," Joe whispered to his sister. "He's scared."

"I know. And now he's up too high." They hadn't practiced a takeoff from a spot so elevated yet.

Oblivious to the kids' conversation, Medici absent-mindedly tapped his fingers on his legs in time with the drumroll Rongo was beating out. "Big finish, you always have to have a big finish." His eyes were glued to the stage.

With a final push, two clowns got Dumbo up onto the platform with them. Holt whistled from below and Dumbo shot the water out of his trunk right onto the burning window.

Backstage, one of the crew members dialed down the flames with a control as Medici pumped his fist in joy. Barrymore, the monkey, leapt through the window onto Dumbo's head and—*mwah!*—gave him a big kiss. Then the rescued monkey scampered down the ramp. The two clowns up top patted each other on the back and pretended not to notice as the men below unhitched the ramp and swung it away.

Whirling to where the ramp had been, the clowns flailed madly, then slipped off the platform, plummeting to the pool below. The crowd cheered.

Alone, Dumbo shifted his weight from foot to foot. Someone was supposed to bring the ramp back now. Instead, the clowns had gotten into a brawl.

"Oh, dear," Medici muttered. "They're improvising. Stay on script!"

Dumbo peered over the edge of the platform.

"Okay, guys, let's get him down." Holt tried to break up the fight. But the other clowns were caught up in their act, throwing and dodging punches, flipping over the edge of the pool and whacking each other with the ladder.

One of the clowns ripped off his helmet and flung it at another, but the second clown ducked, so the hat went sailing offstage . . . right toward the fire controls. The stagehand dove aside and the helmet crashed into the dial, knocking it off the board.

*Whoosh!* Flames burst out around the window next to Dumbo again. But he didn't have any water to put them out! Skittering backward, his foot kicked the bar the ramp latched onto, sending it askew.

"Guys!" Holt hissed at the clowns.

Suddenly aware of their surroundings, the clowns burst into action, raising the ramp to the platform. But without a bar, they couldn't secure it. The ladder slipped back to smash across the pool.

"Wooooo!" the audience cried happily, thinking it was all part of the act.

Holt raced to the curtained-off section. "Max, he's trapped up there!" How were they going to get him down? They needed to clear the tent, maybe get a net set up or some kind of crane? Holt's mind whirled.

"Get that fire OUT!" Medici bellowed.

The stagehand was doing his best to reattach the dial and another rushed off to find a wrench to see if they could force it. Up on the platform, the flames leapt from the window frame and licked the platform boards and support poles. Dumbo shrank back as far as he could, nearly toppling off the edge.

"Dumbo, please! Why won't he fly?" Joe asked. The poor guy was scared to death! His eyes were rolling back in his head. What if he fainted and fell off?

Milly fiddled with the key around her neck, then spotted Ivan and Catherine's box of mourning doves. "Joe, he needs his feather! He won't fly without a feather."

Quick as a flash, Joe darted over and snatched a fallen feather from the bottom of the birdcage and hustled it back to Milly.

Milly clutched the feather and burst through the curtains, heading across the ring to where the clowns were desperately trying to lean the ladder ramp against the other side of the platform. "Dumbo, we're coming!" she shouted.

"Milly! What are you doing?" Holt hurried after her, but she was already leaping onto the ladder and scrambling up.

"I thought she didn't want an act," Medici mumbled as he hurried onstage to help.

Dumbo trumpeted as Milly poked her head above the platform. His hairs were starting to curl from the heat.

"Here, show them, Dumbo! Show the whole world what you can do. For Mom." Milly held the feather out to him.

His eyes sparkled and his trunk curled around the feather.

*Crack!*

Boards on the platform splintered and the ladder swung wildly.

"Aaah!" Milly dangled from the side, the floor below her spinning. Her father held up his arm as though he could catch her, then cursed his missing limb.

"Oh, no!" The audience gasped, finally realizing this was not part of the act.

There—the pool was below her. She could do it. She had to. Unfurling her fingers, Milly dropped.

*Splash!* Water covered her head and she spluttered to the surface as a hand gripped her shirt and hauled her to the edge of the pool, pulling her to her father's side.

"Are you okay?" Holt asked.

Milly choked out a yes, but her eyes were fixed on the platform above. More loud cracks reverberated through the tent as the planks began to separate. With nowhere to go, Dumbo fell.

"Dumbo, fly! Fly!" Milly shouted.

In midair, Dumbo inhaled the feather. With a snap, his ears spread wide and flapped once, twice.

*Zoom!* Dumbo soared up. Up toward the ceiling, up past the broken platform, up over the heads of the crowd. Round the tent he went, flapping with joy.

The teenage boys who'd been taunting him before yelled out again, calling him a freak. Dumbo steered toward the pool and sucked up some water with his trunk. On his next pass, he sprayed the boys.

"Eek!" the teens shrieked as the rest of the crowd laughed. Both in the ring and backstage, the performers were frozen in shock. Rongo's hands hung motionless over the instruments, so the only sounds were the cries of the audience as they ducked for cover and the *flap-flap* of Dumbo's ears.

"Woo-hoo! Yes!" Milly cheered.

Holt stared down at his drenched daughter. "You *knew* he could do this?"

Milly just smiled and high-fived Joe, who'd come out from backstage as well.

Medici and Holt stared at one another.

"Please start talking to your kids," Medici said.

Slowly, the crowd realized Dumbo wasn't going to plow into them. They cheered him on, whooping and clapping as he zoomed through the air. Dumbo's smile widened, and his eyes shone brightly. Veering left, he looped again and again, spiraling down, then up, then down again.

Every eye was trained on him as he dove and rose and curved like a paintbrush on the air. This was magic, real magic, happening right there in Joplin, Missouri.

By the next day, word had zipped down phone wires and been pressed onto newspapers: THE MEDICI BROTHERS HAVE A FLYING PACHYDERM!

Ticket sales for the show would no longer be a concern.

The newest addition to the Medici circus—the little elephant called Dumbo—had saved them.

* * *

Far, far away, in New York City, businessman V. A. Vandevere slapped down his copy of the paper.

"Sotheby," he called to his personal assistant, "pack our bags. We have business in Missouri."

If the story was true, the Medici Brothers had an elephant that could literally fly. It seemed impossible, and yet V. A. made a business out of making the impossible possible.

That elephant belonged in his circus. . . .

He just had to go fetch it.

# CHAPTER
## TEN

crowd clamored outside the closed Medici Bros. Circus ticket booth. In his tiny office inside the circus train's caboose, Medici rubbed his hands gleefully, then plastered on a friendly yet reluctant expression and walked out to address them.

"My friends, *grazie mille*, it's a limited engagement!" He shrugged apologetically as he pointed to the signs pasted in the ticket booth window that read SOLD-OUT PERFORMANCES: TODAY/TOMORROW/NEXT DAY, TOO!

Ripples of dismay ran through the crowd and Medici raised his arms to quiet them down. "Next available shows are in Arkansas! However, I am

127

offering a chance at a once-in-a-lifetime keepsake: your photograph with Dumbo, the amazing flying elephant! An absolute steal at three?—two?—I'm descended from saints—*one* dollar a pop!"

He grinned broadly at everyone, silently calculating how many people were there and how much money that translated into.

"Line up here. We open in an hour, folks!"

With a jaunty wave, he headed through the circus. His performers' spirits soared like Dumbo himself, everyone turned into giddy dreamers by the miraculous animal among them.

"Hah! Yeah!" The clowns called as they danced in front of their tent, feet whirling through the sand. Linking arms, they spun like a tornado, faster and faster.

"Hurrah!" Medici shouted to them. "That's the spirit! Let's astound and amaze like we used to do."

Across the way, Rongo hefted Miss Atlantis over his head, muscles bunching.

Medici did a double take. "Rongo, what's gotten into you? Using real weights again—I love it!" He tipped his hat to them both and sauntered on. Up ahead, Catherine snuggled on Ivan's lap, their fingers weaving together as they laughed at a private joke.

"That's what your magic's been missing. *Bellisimo,*

*vero amore!*" Eyes twinkling, Medici left them in peace. Dumbo was the best thing that had happened to his circus. Now he would be world-famous! Not to mention set for life.

He'd reached his destination: a small green-and-white-striped tent. DUMBO, THE FANTASTIC FLYING ELEPHANT! proclaimed the sign in front.

Inside, a photographer waited off to the side, double-checking his equipment as Medici's crew painted a blue sky studded with clouds on a large backdrop. Two more men were stretching and squishing cotton stuffing into a puffball around the pedestal where Dumbo would stand. Medici could see it now: Dumbo's ears flared wide, adoring fans clustered close as the camera went *flash!* Floating above them would be Barrymore, dressed as an angel.

Barrymore was not pleased.

Puck coaxed the monkey into the rope harness, but he kept swatting at the halo attached to his head. "Shhh, shhh, it's all right, it's just a wire circle," Puck said soothingly.

*Pppfft.* Barrymore stuck his tongue out at his trainer.

"Will you tell him it's heaven? I need him to sell it," Medici said. "Gimme the Sistine Chapel, but with class."

*"Ooo-ooo-weeeaahh-weeeah!"* the little monkey screeched, and flung its prop harp at Puck.

"Oh, dear." Medici spun away. Puck would work it out with the monkey. "Now where is my star?"

\* \* \*

Next door, Holt supervised Dumbo's bath. The elephant preened as a few of the acrobats scrubbed behind his ears. Warm water tickled his tummy and soapy bubbles kept him endlessly entertained. He kept them aloft with little puffs from his trunk.

Milly and Joe giggled as Dumbo blinked at another bubble's splash on his trunk. Holt shared a smile with Pramesh. The snake charmer and his nephew had followed Dumbo almost everywhere since his performance, bringing him bushels of grass, sweet fruits, and flowers for his pen.

"In our country, legends tell us that the gods once took animal forms," Pramesh said softly.

"Ah, Dumbo," Medici boomed as he bustled into the tent. "How's your bath? Too warm? Too cold?" Medici tested the water with his hand, then ran his fingers down Dumbo's back. "Girls, make sure his wrinkles don't get wrinkles."

Laughing, the acrobats splashed Dumbo, who

130

sprayed them back. Then he bolted upright, his ears swooping out to their fullest.

Holt wondered what Dumbo was so excited about. All he could hear was the purr of a car's engine outside.

*Boom!* The sides of the clown pool burst as Dumbo charged out. Water doused Medici, and the acrobats, swept off their feet, slipped to the ground.

"Remind me to look into insurance," Medici said, wringing out his shirt.

Not pausing to look back, Dumbo tore out of the tent, Milly and Joe hot on his tail.

\* \* \*

Outside, Dumbo peered around eagerly. Milly and Joe came up beside him—they had a pretty good idea what he was looking for, but the engine noise wasn't from Brugelbecker's truck. Just a long, sleek silver car slowing to a stop next to the circus's entrance.

Dumbo's ears drooped and he sat back on his haunches.

"I'm sorry, Dumbo. It's not your mama." Milly rubbed the back of his head.

"Who *is* it?" Joe asked. It must be someone rich to own a car that fancy. How many people could fit inside it?

"That's V. A. Vandevere," his father said, his voice full of awe.

Medici tumbled out to join them. "Vandevere!" The circus director's face paled. "Quick, back into the tent, Dumbo." Medici urged the elephant inside.

Joe shot him a curious look, but the lure of the newcomers was stronger. He followed his dad and sister to the front entrance as though drawn to the car by a magnet.

\* \* \*

Medici breathed a sigh of relief once Dumbo was back inside the tent. The elephant looked somewhat dejected, but he perked up when Pramesh presented him with an orange. According to Joe, Dumbo had learned how to squish them with his feet and suck up the juicy bits with his trunk, transferring them to his mouth. But Medici couldn't stay to watch this time. There could only be one reason for the business tycoon V. A. Vandevere to visit Medici's circus . . . and it wasn't a good one.

Medici hurried out of the tent to greet the visitors.

A broad-shouldered man with narrow eyes and a sour expression stepped out of the car first. He scanned the crowd outside the gate and the ragtag circus tents beyond.

"Ah, Sotheby. We're a long way from nowhere," he muttered to his companion, who was just emerging.

"Yes, quite, Skellig," the second man spoke, his words coated in a formal English accent

From what Medici could tell, Sotheby was all cool aplomb, while his counterpart, Skellig, was rough-and-tumble. Sotheby surveyed the scene, then cleared his throat.

"Ladies and gentlemen," he announced to the group, stepping forward, "please make way for the emperor of enchantment, the architect of dreams, Mr. V. A. Vandevere!" One arm swooped back toward the car.

Out stepped a third man—a handsome gentleman in a gray three-piece suit, smiling benevolently as though he were the king of Missouri. His nose was straight, his teeth even straighter and sparkling white. Keen blue eyes, the color of the sky, took in the field of yellow grass and the dilapidated circus at its center.

"And traveling with him, his bright shining star: Colette Marchant, the Queen of the Heavens!" the British man proclaimed.

Vandevere held out his hand, and gloved fingers extended from the car, followed by a stunning woman whose dress glittered with sequins, and whose wiry

shoulders were cloaked with a fur cape trimmed in feathers. Her smile was dazzling as she tossed her curled ebony hair. With her fine cheekbones and air of mystery, Medici thought she would have made a great fortune-teller, but of course, her petite, athletic frame spoke of graceful acrobatics.

Vandevere and Colette cut through the crowd smoothly, pausing to pose for photos and sign autographs as the crowd clamored to brush against the celebrities.

"Now that's how you make an entrance," Holt told his kids.

Vandevere and his companions made it through to the circus gate, where Medici and the others waited.

"Ah, Signor Medici," Vandevere said.

Medici leaned in to Holt and hissed, "He knows who I am!" Puffing up his chest as the legendary Vandevere approached, he nodded in greeting.

"Just passing through Missouri," the taller man drawled. "Heard you were putting on a show."

"Mr. Vandevere, it's an honor." Medici shook his hand, feeling out of his depth but trying not to let it show.

"No, the honor's mine," Vandevere answered.

"Come, let's talk in my office," Medici said, waving the newcomers to the caboose. He jerked his head at

Holt to go back to Dumbo. There wouldn't be room in the train car for everyone.

Sure enough, it was a tight fit as Skellig and Sotheby followed Vandevere, Colette, and Medici into the caboose. Skellig took up a position by a wall, while Sotheby hovered in the doorway. Vandevere settled into a wooden chair as though it were a comfy pillow. Colette glanced around the paper-strewn space, searching for another seat.

"Sit, sit, take a load off," Medici said, scooping pamphlets and a couple of top hats off another chair and dumping them all on a footstool behind his desk. He slipped on a jacket over his shirt, which was still soaked from Dumbo's splashing, and rubbed his hands together. "Now, who'd like a drink? Though I'm all out of bourbon. And brandy. And Scotch," Medici rattled off. Did he have anything?!

He pulled open the drawer where he kept his reserve stash.

*"Neeeaahh! Ksssss!"* Barrymore suddenly appeared, hissing at Medici, his tiny paws gripping Medici's silver flask tightly.

Colette jumped and Skellig leaned in to get a closer look, but Sotheby and Vandevere were unruffled.

"Aargh! Not now," Medici scolded as he tried to slam the drawer shut.

"Is that a monkey in your desk?" Vandevere asked calmly.

"Just for emergencies." Medici wrestled the drawer shut and plonked down on his desk chair. "Also, I should probably mention, the elephant is not for sale. We're already sold out at the next five stops."

"Mmm. You're welcome, Max. Who do you think bought half the tickets?"

Medici's eyes nearly popped out of his head. He knew Vandevere had deep pockets, but to buy out half the shows for the next two months? That was unheard-of money. Still, he couldn't imagine an amount that would get him to part with Dumbo.

Barrymore rattled inside the drawer, rocking the desk up and down. Fed up, Medici thumped the top of the desk with his fist, and the monkey finally quieted. Now maybe Medici could think.

"Wouldn't want your new act to be overexposed at such a critical time," Vandevere continued.

"Uh-huh. Well, I wouldn't want to waste your time. The elephant will only fly for the Medici Circus. Only for me and my talented trainer." Medici shrugged, as if he regretted he couldn't be of more help. The faster he got Vandevere out of there, the better, he thought.

"That's assuming he is real," Colette cut in smoothly. Medici detected an accent—was she French?

Perhaps French-Canadian? She plucked a dollar from her purse and dropped it on Medici's desk. "One dollar for a photograph, yes?"

Medici shrugged and pocketed the coin. If they wanted to see Dumbo, so be it. The only trace of Dumbo they'd leave with would be a photo.

# CHAPTER
## ELEVEN

ven through the clothespin on his nose, Holt could smell the nauseating scent of elephant dung. Thankfully, Dumbo was a quarter the size of the other two, although he still managed to produce an awful lot of dung. Holt awkwardly scraped the shovel along the floor and strong-armed it up and into a wheelbarrow.

Joe, who was supposed to be helping him, laughed as Dumbo tickled him. Holt didn't have the heart to interrupt. He wished again he knew how to make his kids happy. Milly was threading short wooden poles through the edge of two yellow flags. What she intended to do with them, Holt had no clue.

Footsteps sounded outside and Holt could hear Medici prattling on about the circus and how much they had to do to get ready for that night. Vandevere was coming.

Before Holt could hide the shovelful of dung, Medici appeared with the legend himself, Colette, and his other two companions.

"With all due respect, I don't got all day. See for yourself. He's as real as rivets," Medici said. His mouth twisted into a frown as Colette swept toward the elephant.

Holt and his shovel were right in her path.

"Um," he mumbled, trying to shift the shovel.

"Excuse me. Watch the dress," she said, lifting the sequins-covered hem off the hay.

Holt spun, shovel out straight, nearly smacking into Skellig, who now lounged in the doorway. Turning once more, Holt found himself face to face with Vandevere, shovel hovering between them like a handshake.

Brain kicking into gear, Holt chucked the shovel to the edge of the tent and quickly wiped his hand along his shirt before presenting it to Vandevere. "Real pleasure to—"

Vandevere glided around him without so much as a second glance, his eyes fixed on the baby elephant.

Colette leaned down to Joe and Milly's eye level. *"Bonjour, enfants,"* she said. "My name's Colette. So. This creature of yours is supposed to *fly*?"

Holt could understand her dubiousness—while Dumbo's ears were impressive, it was hard to believe a creature that large could get off the ground.

Nodding, Milly gave her an eager smile, then stretched her new flags overhead. Dumbo's ears perked up tall, then copied Milly's move as she snapped the flags down again. As the resulting wind pushed against her, Colette stepped back . . . right onto Holt's shovel. She glared at him.

Vandevere eyed Dumbo like a predator observing its prey. Medici rushed forward and snatched up the flags from Milly.

"Come on, kid, trade secrets," he hissed.

"May I ask where you obtained the elephant?" Vandevere's voice was as slick as a puddle of oil.

"I'm not at liberty to say," Medici hedged. "He hails from the Far East."

"How far?"

"Far." Medici's chin jutted out like it always did when he was feeling annoyed.

"He does not look 'magic' to me," Skellig chimed in.

Holt bristled. "Well, what the heck can you tell by appearances?" He swiped his hat off Joe's head and plopped it onto his own before moving to Vandevere's side again. "Hello, sir. Holt Farrier. You might have heard of my Stallion Stars? It's a horse act, a great one."

Of course his fake arm chose that moment to slide down and hang loosely at his side. Vandevere raised his eyebrows at it.

"*Pfft*, Germans." Holt waved with his other hand, feeling his face flush. "Just a scratch."

Colette found a rake and began scraping her shoe off along the spikes. A few blue feathers on her hem furled up with the movement. Dumbo zeroed in on them and his trunk inched out, grazing Colette's knee. She quickly drew back.

"And you train flying elephants, too?" she asked Holt, studying Dumbo's flanks.

Holt could guess what she was looking for—marks from whatever wires or harness she thought they used. She'd be flabbergasted if she knew the truth.

"Little hobby, on the side," Holt answered.

"Actually," Medici said, "it's his kids who taught Dumbo his talent." Medici grinned as Holt glared at him. His eyes seemed to challenge Holt: *Go ahead, see if you can wow him.*

Vandevere's gaze swung to the kids. "The children. Fascinating. And how on earth did you do that?" he asked Milly.

141

"With the scientific method," she said proudly.

Medici edged in front of her. "Ah-ah. They don't understand English."

"So how long are you staying?" Holt asked.

Medici rolled his eyes. "For one picture, *one* picture."

The photographer jumped forward at Medici's wave.

"Ah, Max, you have something that is very rare in life." Vandevere's tone was reverent. "And the tragedy is that you don't even realize that you have it. Do you know what you have?"

"Migraines?" Medici quipped. He needed Vandevere gone before the Farriers gave away any more secrets.

"Mystique . . ." Vandevere said. "Until the moment you sell its picture."

*Crash.* Skellig knocked over the photographer's camera, which smashed to bits on the dirt floor.

"Hey!" the photographer shouted.

Holt cringed and Medici's eyebrows pulled together in a stern frown. The photographer charged a steep price, and the camera must have been even more expensive—something they couldn't really afford in the first place. Skellig looked at Holt as if challenging him to object.

Instead, Holt bent to gather all the sharp broken glass. Apart from Dumbo's safety, he knew his kids played in there barefoot. The last thing he wanted was someone getting injured.

"Come take a walk with me, Max. I think you'll want to hear what I have to say," Vandevere said.

* * *

Dust swirled up from the dry ground of the meadow outside the circus, choking Medici. He waved it off in annoyance, glancing up at Vandevere.

"Max, trust me, I know your kind." Vandevere smiled down condescendingly. "Charlatan, con man, opportunist—"

*Nope*, Medici thought. He had not come out here to be insulted. "Uh-huh. New York's that way; happy to give you directions."

Vandevere held up his hands placatingly. "But I also know it comes from a deep desire to one day build something authentic and true." He pulled a silver coin from his pocket and tossed it in the air.

"I know your game," Medici said. He'd met plenty of men like Vandevere—all out to scoop up more power and money, not caring who they trampled in the process. Plus, he knew this magic trick.

"It's not a game." Vandevere wound the coin

through his fingers. "Some men cheat rules. Others change them."

With a final toss, the coin arced into the air, and then Vandevere grabbed it and unfurled his palm to reveal it was empty. The coin was gone.

Medici folded his arms and shot Vandevere a disgusted look. "It's up your sleeve."

"It's in your pocket," Vandevere countered.

Medici patted his jacket and found a folded piece of paper. Drawing it out, he nearly lost his footing. The check covered more than a year's worth of expenses for the circus, and the note attached claimed something Medici had never expected.

"Secret to show business, my friend," Vandevere continued as Medici read everything over again. "Always keep a rabbit in your hat. Or a monkey in your desk, I suppose."

"Ownership shares?" Medici tilted his head and studied Vandevere. Was this real? Vandevere wanted him to be part owner of the Dreamland circus?

"Max, look around. Your whole way of life is ending."

Medici gazed at his life's work—the patched tents, the scrappy crew sawing new cutouts or practicing their acts despite being half the number they used to be. Every loss had cut Medici's heart—he considered the troupe his family, and whether it was due to death or disbanding, he hated that the family was shrinking instead of growing. They hadn't had anyone new join them in over a year. Maybe Vandevere was right—circuses no longer held the same allure.

"The future of entertainment is getting the whole world to travel to *you*. I have built that destination, but what I lack"—Vandevere paused and turned soulful eyes on Medici—"is a protégé."

Was Vandevere saying what he thought he was saying? Medici scratched his head absently, forgetting there was a check in his hand until the paper hit his forehead.

"I know there's no Medici 'brothers.' You probably always wanted one." Vandevere looked sincere.

"You're offering me a *partnership*?" Medici asked.

Vandevere nodded. "And a home. For your entire troupe." He spread his arms wide. "No more traveling, debt, or struggle. We'll all soar on that elephant's wings. Or ears. However it works."

Medici's eyes rested on his circus, where his performers and crew were waiting for him. "A home for *all* of us?"

"Join with me and my family in Dreamland and let me take us all into the future." Vandevere's face was aglow as he spoke of Dreamland.

Caught up in Vandevere's enthusiasm, Medici pictured them working side by side, transforming Dreamland into *the* premier circus in the world. People would travel to them, and without all the setup, transit, and breakdown costs, Medici could invest more in props and costumes, build permanent stages . . . The possibilities were endless.

"All right. Partners," Medici proclaimed, sticking out his hand.

Vandevere grinned as they shook. He seemed just as genuinely excited as Medici.

There would be paperwork to lay out all the details.

But Dumbo and the whole Medici family would be moving to Dreamland.

Where all their dreams would come true.

# MEDICI
## PITTSBURGH,
## PENNSYLVANIA, 1887

No, Max Medici didn't have a twin brother—or a brother at all, for that matter. Max Medici wasn't even his real name. He was born Gustavo Jakub Klosinski. But he was smart enough to know a catchy hook was needed in the circus business. And if there was one thing Max excelled at above all others, it was drawing people in. A salesman of marvels, a peddler of curiosities, a born entertainer. He knew how to make a crowd gasp and shiver with excitement. From the age of five, he cracked jokes in the kitchen while his mother and aunts scrubbed laundry until they waved him off. At eight, he drove his teachers crazy as he interrupted lessons, wanting every eye fixed on him.

When his father disappeared, eleven-year-old Max dropped out of school and set up shop as a shoeshine, spinning tall tales for his customers. Some people would come back, transfixed, while others found him too forward and took their business elsewhere. But day by day, Max practiced how to catch and hold a person's interest.

*Then, when he was thirteen, a circus arrived in Pittsburgh.*

*"Bernardo, wait for me," he called after his best friend.*

*Up ahead, Bernardo paused impatiently by the lamp-post until Gustavo reached him.*

*"Gustavo, you have to keep up," Bernardo scolded. "That was the deal."*

*"I can't help it. My legs are shorter than yours." He kept hoping for a growth spurt.*

*As they turned onto the drive leading to the circus, they could see the tall tents ahead, lights and streamers strung between them.*

*His stomach felt fizzy.*

*"Ugh," Bernardo groaned. "How are we going to get in? Look at that line."*

*"Never fear, 'Nardo. Where there is a will, there is a way." Gustavo led him around to the side, where a make-shift fence surrounded the fair.*

*Prying apart two flat sections, the kids slipped inside. A white sheet of fabric met them—they were behind a small tent. Edging around it, they saw a cook fire and benches set up all around it—this must be where the circus performers ate. Gustavo pictured them all coming offstage, roaring with laughter and slapping each other* on the back as they settled in to eat and talk and joke with one another. A family not of blood, but of friendship and camaraderie.

Bernardo hustled forward, knocking Gustavo's imagination back to the present. Quickly, he caught up to his friend, and they both eased into the crowd along the main thoroughfare, where the sideshow booths were set up.

"Whoa!" Bernardo pointed to a man on a pedestal juggling lighted torches.

The next person over wasn't all that strange. Sure, she had more facial hair than the usual woman, but Gustavo had seen plenty of almost-full mustaches on his older female relatives. Still, the kids stopped to watch as the bearded lady spun in a circle and tugged on her hair so they'd know it was real.

"Look at that!" Bernardo nudged Gustavo and led him to a pair of contortionists who were twisted together, their limbs looking like a pretzel.

The boys swiped some popcorn, and after half an hour of wandering, they made it to the main tent. Applause thundered as the previous act ended. The benches were packed, but Gustavo found them standing spots near the front.

Lights flashed, spotlights dancing around the tent

*while someone tapped out a drumroll.* Bang! *went the cymbal. The lights veered to the center of the ring, where an elegantly dressed man in a top hat and tails bowed.*

*"You've seen feats of strength and speed. Now be dazzled by our most daring duo—the Leaping Leonardos!"*

*Swooping away, the spotlights illuminated two men in sparkling green leotards standing on platforms at least fifty feet off the floor, facing each other. Each waved to the crowd, then stepped forward and unhooked a bar between two ropes.*

*"Those are trapezes," Gustavo whispered to Bernardo, acting like an expert when he'd only just heard the word from the people nearest them.*

*"I know," his friend huffed.*

*Dangling from their hands, the two men pushed off, swinging out over open air. Gustavo gasped, then noticed the net below, its black threads camouflaged in the darkness. Still, how brave of those performers! Now one was hanging upside down by his knees. The other suddenly let go of his trapeze!*

*Gustavo's stomach clenched, his eyes riveted on the man.*

*The acrobat tucked into a ball, spinning through the air like a hoop, before extending his body out into a straight line, reaching for his partner. They linked arms, the trapeze holding them both whooshing even faster.*

*For the rest of the performance, Gustavo didn't move. Even when the lights came up and everyone was ushered out, he stood, immobile in the press of people exiting. Bernardo tugged on his arm, but instead of heading for the exit, Gustavo plunged into the ring itself.*

*A burly crewman busy hoisting down the nets yelled at him to stop.*

*The ringmaster appeared at Gustavo's side. "Who are you?" he asked, not angrily.*

*"My name is Gustavo Jakub Klosinski."*

*"Can I help you?"*

*"Yes, please!" Gustavo nearly tripped over his words.*

*"With what?"*

*"How do I become you?"*

*The man studied Gustavo's hopeful upturned face, the fervor in his eyes. "Ah, caught the circus bug, have you? It's a hard one to shake, I have to warn you. If you let it in further, it will take over your life, consume your every waking minute . . . and dollar."*

*"Where do I start?" Gustavo asked.*

*The man laughed. "Sign on as a stagehand, learn the trade. Or rustle up enough money to start your own show from scratch." The man winked. He was clearly joking about that last one—circuses must have been very expensive.*

*Gustavo nodded thoughtfully. "Thank you, thank*

you." He shook the man's hand and turned to go. Bernardo fidgeted a few feet away.

"Hey, Gustavo," the ringmaster called after him.

Gustavo looked back at the ringmaster.

"Whatever you do, change your name!"

Hmmm. *It was true. It would be hard to spread word of mouth about a traveling circus if nobody could pronounce—or spell—the name.*

*As Gustavo followed Bernardo back to their neighborhood, the streets of Pittsburgh blurred around him. Visions of acrobats and clowns, freaks and unusual acts danced through his mind. And at the center of them all, he stood in a spotlight, proudly waving to an audience of cheering men, women, and children.*

*One day, he would make it happen. All of it.*

*He'd run the greatest circus there ever was.*

# CHAPTER
# TWELVE

## NEW YORK CITY, 1920

Two months later, after all the contracts had been reviewed and signed, arrangements made, tour dates cancelled, tickets refunded with promises of discounts if customers traveled to Dreamland to see Dumbo's act . . . after the circus had been packed up and loaded onto the train for the last time, Milly, Joe, and Holt pressed their noses against the glass of the train's window.

"There it is!" Milly gasped at the high buildings reaching skyward like teetering acrobats when they piled up on each other's shoulders. "Can you believe it?"

"New York City," Joe marveled. "Center of the world!"

Chugging over bridges, the train passed crowded apartment buildings with folks hanging over the rooftop ledges to get a peek at them, while others strolled down wide avenues, parasols lifted to shield their faces from the sun. Milly had never seen so many cars jockeying for position on the roads. The calls of hawkers selling their goods, newsboys, horn blasts, and engine noise filled the air. As they rolled away from Manhattan, the houses grew shorter, but were just as packed together. Milly sniffed—salt! They were near the ocean.

Slowly, the Medici train pulled into the final station, the end of the line. Milly and Joe bounded out, followed by their father. They couldn't believe they were finally there. From all they'd heard, Dreamland was a wondrous place. In the distance they could see the soaring ring of a Ferris wheel and the curving line of a roller coaster. In the center, rising above a set of swirling metal gates, was a delicate tower. The letters "V.A.V." were spelled out in lights on its side, and a glass-enclosed room near the top promised an incredible view of the circus and the sea below.

"Ah, welcome!" Vandevere strode down the train platform and pumped Medici's hand. Colette, draped in a peacock blue capelet, trailed behind him, waving hello to the kids.

When she'd first seen her, Milly had been intimidated by Colette, sure this elegant lady would frown at Milly's patchwork jumpsuit attire—not to mention her outlandish notions of training Dumbo using the scientific method. But Colette's warmth felt genuine. She seemed honestly curious about Milly and her ideas.

"I trust you've had a safe journey. I've made arrangements for Dumbo, as you can see." Vandevere interrupted Milly's thoughts, pointing to a giant gold-encrusted covered carriage drawn by horses. It featured a small barred window at the back. Several of his men backed it up close to the train and quickly loaded the little elephant into it.

"Wait," Milly called. She ducked inside Dumbo's boxcar on the train and emerged with the mouse circus. "These are his friends; he likes to have them close by." She carefully tucked the cage into the carriage and patted Dumbo on the trunk.

"Now, follow me to our own ride," Vandevere said to the Farriers, Medici, and Colette as the men closed up the carriage. He led them to the silver car they'd seen before, now with its top down. Sotheby held the door open as Milly, Joe, and Holt piled into the back. Vandevere, Colette, and Medici took the front row, and Sotheby slid behind the wheel.

The car rolled smoothly up to a massive curved gate that marked the entrance to Dreamland in a flourish of letters. Milly held her breath as it swung slowly open. She gazed around as the car passed inside. Directly ahead of them, a line of booths and flashy attractions led to a massive, elaborate tent. But unlike their own traveling tent, this one had metal pillars and railings for the attached fabric, and it was five times the size. Off to their left lay amusement park rides, like the Ferris wheel and a roller coaster. A rocket ship appeared to soar above. Shrieks of delight came from that area. Yet Milly's gaze was drawn to the right, where sleek, modern buildings announced the future. One was emblazoned with words she'd never imagined.

"Look, Dad! 'Wonders of Science,'" she read aloud, pointing to the building with electric wires zigzagging above it. Her whole body tingled as though gentle waves of electricity were flowing over her.

"Slow down, sugarplum," Holt cautioned. "We have

a job to do here." Vandevere was watching Milly with curiosity. "My daughter fancies herself the next Marie Curie," Holt told him.

Vandevere tilted his head, studying Milly. He smiled. "I once overheard my father say I'd never amount to anything. Now he calls me every year asking for money." His intense gaze focused on Milly alone. "Never let *anyone* tell you what you can't do," he said fiercely.

"Hang on, I wasn't saying—" Holt spluttered, clearly upset at being painted as unsupportive. He loved Milly with all his heart; he just wanted something practical for her future rather than crushed dreams of a world beyond reach. He knew what it was like to lose things that were precious to him. He wanted to protect her from that hurt.

Vandevere didn't wait for Holt to finish. He motioned lazily and they continued on toward the large tent. Crowds of people lined the path, cheering and waving as the procession rolled past.

"Have you ever seen so many people?" Milly asked.

"I know. I wish Mom could have seen it." Joe looked wistful.

Regaining his composure, Holt smiled at his kids. "Somehow, I think she knows we're here." Then he leaned forward and whispered to Medici, "Way to work your magic, Gustavo."

"Shhh." Medici waved him off.

"*Eeeeaaauuugh?*" A plaintive call came from the carriage. Milly and Joe twisted to see it behind them.

"It's okay! We hear you, Dumbo," Milly called. "Why won't you let him see outside?" Dumbo loved waving to people, but the carriage only had the small barred window, too high up for him to peek out of. She was sure he wanted to know what all the commotion was.

"Patience, young lady. *Mystique*," Vandevere explained.

*  *  *

Behind the carriage, the rest of Medici's circus brought up the end of the parade, their faces full of awe. They'd never been greeted like this before.

"Now this is why I joined the circus," Rongo said happily.

Miss Atlantis smiled from behind her veiled hat while Pramesh and his nephew nodded their heads at the clamoring crowd. Catherine blew kisses to the spectators while Ivan waved like a movie star. Puck straightened his back, puffing up his chest, prompting

Rongo to elbow him playfully. The clowns broke out into spontaneous cartwheels and somersaults while the acrobats glided along gracefully.

* * *

Tires crunched to a stop as they pulled up in front of the main tent.

Vandevere turned toward his masterpiece of a circus, putting a hand on Colette's shoulder. "Here it is, the center of it all! What is it that we do here, *ma chérie*?"

Colette knew her cue. She threw back her arms and beamed. "We make the impossible possible!"

Gazing around, Milly believed it. Everything looked brand-new and shiny.

"And that's where you'll perform: the Colosseum!" Sotheby pointed to the enormous tent, which Milly now noticed was decorated with six-foot-tall banners featuring Colette. They'd never seen a tent with such angles—the stadium beneath it was permanent, with sleek metal support beams. "Training tents are behind it. That's where Dumbo will stay."

Skellig and several men steered the horses off in that direction, golden carriage bumping along behind them. A nervous trumpet leaked out.

"We're here, Dumbo! Don't worry!" Joe called back.

"Why aren't we going with him?" Milly asked. Dumbo liked to have her and Joe settle him in, and they usually slept nearby these days.

"Because we're headed to your new home."

* * *

A little while later, Vandevere strode toward a beautiful building on the edge of the circus and unlocked the oak front door.

Holt and his kids blinked. They weren't sleeping in a tent anymore? No more chilly nights and stifling hot afternoons? No more tiptoeing around each other's cots in the middle of the night to use the bathroom?

Vandevere stood waiting in the doorway. The Farriers hurried to follow him inside, Medici and Colette tagging along. Joe raced up a set of stairs, tearing across parquet floors and through velvet-curtained rooms. Milly hoped he wouldn't accidentally knock over a priceless antique or crash into a window.

"Look at this place!" Joe bounded outside to a balcony that overlooked the whole park.

Milly found the bedrooms—she'd have her own! One of them had a floor-to-ceiling wall of books and a bed that was made up with yellow-flowered sheets. Walking over to the shelves, she caressed the spines of the books. "A library . . . in my room." Her heart felt like it was exploding. Until now she'd only been able to keep a handful of books at a time. Packing light had always been an important part of traveling with the circus.

She took it all in—the yellow swirling pattern on the floors, the emerald green curtains framing giant windows. It was like they had just made it to Oz.

Vandevere drank in the children's expressions. "And the children shall lead them," he whispered softly.

* * *

*What does that mean?* Holt wondered, studying Vandevere. The businessman's lips curved up in a half smile. Shrugging, Holt decided not to ask. He didn't want to come across as ignorant.

"We're all very grateful for the opportunity, sir," Holt said. The house was incredible. Even after a lifetime of work, Holt would never have been able to buy a place like this. He could hardly believe it. It felt too good to be true.

"Of course. Your family is mine." Vandevere's eyebrows twitched. "If you'd like to settle in later, there's something on the grounds I'd like to share with you."

After this place, Holt couldn't wait to see what

else Dreamland held. He nodded and ushered his kids out of the house—they could explore all its nooks and crannies that night.

Vandevere led the group to a grand scarlet-colored tent with golden trim. Inside the tent, in the middle of a packed-dirt ring, were twelve beautiful horses, each with a handler. Holt's heart squeezed. Their coats varied from bright white to honey palomino, chestnut, and dark bay, with one bold pinto perfect for a cowboy. Even more impressive, there were two Arabians, their delicate heads and graceful necks arching as they pranced in place.

"I brushed up on your story, Mr. Farrier. You were Kentucky's top trick rider. There's no reason you can't be again." Vandevere waved and a stablehand pulled a rope, releasing a banner.

Against a patriotic backdrop of stars and stripes, a picture of a one-armed rider on a rearing horse stood out.

"Except here, it would be as Captain Farrier: war hero!" Vandevere held out his hands, as though framing the words in midair. "A one-armed wonder, a national treasure. We'll wrap you in a folktale and flag."

*Really?* Holt couldn't believe it. He wouldn't have to pretend here—no fake arm, no mustache or clown's makeup. "I still can ride," Holt said. It was half statement, half question. He glanced at Medici, who'd been so sure Holt's injury would scare people. Judging by his expression, Medici was kicking himself for not having the same vision as Vandevere. Maybe crowds *would* cheer for a returning war hero—perhaps even chant his name.

"I know you can," Vandevere answered.

Holt surveyed the horses.

"And you're going to . . . right after you get the little elephant off the ground for me," Vandevere added.

Ah. So there was the catch.

"You mean, once his act's working . . ." Holt trailed off, wanting to be sure Vandevere was promising what he thought he was.

"You're back in the saddle." The Dreamland owner grinned.

Holt could respect that—good business was always about a fair trade. If he did his job well, he'd get his own act and a chance to be a star again.

Milly and Joe rushed over, hugging their dad tightly, sharing in his excitement.

Vandevere turned to Medici. "Now, we're still working out times for the rest of the troupe, but on Friday we premiere our little Dumbo."

Medici nodded agreeably.

It made sense that the rest of the crew would need to be fitted into Vandevere's existing acts, but Holt could understand his eagerness to show off Dumbo. Who could blame him? Dumbo was incredible.

"Getting goosebumps, *cherie*?" Vandevere asked Colette. For the first time, Holt saw the actress look ruffled. She'd always projected cool confidence and an air of—what was that word Vandevere loved?— *mystique*. Now her eyebrows crinkled and her lips pursed in confusion.

\* \* \*

Colette stared back at Vandevere, baffled. "Why are you looking at me?" Usually she had a fairly good idea what her boss was thinking, but this time she didn't understand the glint in his eye.

"Because the only thing more amazing than a flying elephant . . . is the goddess who is able to fly with it."

"Have you lost your mind?"

Vandevere's eyes stayed on the ceiling, as if he were already seeing Dumbo and Colette soaring past.

Colette knew that face—he was serious. She still doubted the elephant could fly, but even if it could, it would surely drop her.

## CHAPTER TWELVE

"What?" Joe stammered as his sister objected, "Fly *with* Dumbo?"

"I'm not sure that's such a good idea," Medici said. Holt nodded nervously, biting his lip.

*See—everyone who has worked with the elephant agrees. It is impossible,* Colette thought. She cocked an eyebrow at Vandevere.

He met her eyes, and she knew from the fire burning in his that her fate had been sealed. "Dearest Colette, let us not forget from whence we came. You *will* fly on Friday. For me."

Colette silently cursed Vandevere and his stupid "making the impossible possible" mantra. And how dare he bring up her background? Just because he'd discovered her didn't mean he had the right to drive— or fly—her to her death, did it? All for the sake of a dream.

"But Dumbo's never flown with anyone," Holt explained. Colette felt a stab of gratitude mixed with pity—Holt didn't know yet that once Vandevere had his mind set on something, he wouldn't let a little thing like logic ruin his vision.

"Then perhaps, my elephant trainer, we're now clear just how much I need you." Vandevere's gaze was steely, pinning Holt to the spot.

The cowboy war hero looked nervous. Very nervous. *Great,* thought Colette. *Just great. My life is in the hands of this fool?*

Spinning on her heel, she stalked out of the tent. As she reached the sanctuary of her suite, two of her maids bobbed their heads. They were packing up for the night and about to leave.

"Evening, Miss Marchant," one said. "Have you heard about the elephant?" Her green eyes glittered in excitement.

"I can't wait to see it!" the other exclaimed.

*Hmmph.* Colette waved them off and slipped inside her room. Sweet lavender perfume filled the air, nothing like the rank animal tents. She sat in front of her makeup table and carefully unpinned the wig she always wore in public. At last, her head felt free to breathe. She ruffled her short milk-chocolate-colored hair, then froze.

In the mirror, she could see workers outside removing her circus banners—the ones where she was posed on a trapeze. She swiveled and peered out the window, reading the new banner as the men hoisted it up: BELIEVE, it proclaimed, with a dark silhouette of an elephant in flight.

This was ridiculous. Her act was being taken over by a lumbering, ungraceful creature.

"Elephants," Colette muttered in outrage. But there was nothing she could do—Vandevere called the shots. So she'd have to make the best of it. She just hoped that cowboy and his children were decent animal trainers.

# COLETTE

## PARIS, 1912

*Colette had picked the corner carefully, finding one with the smoothest sidewalk possible. The concrete had been poured just the week before, in fact. She might have also been swayed by the fact that there was a bakery there, reminding her of picking up bread for her family each morning in rural France, although the delicious aromas were now making her stomach hurt, and the memories of Maman and Papa were bittersweet. They'd been the ones to introduce her to gymnastics, folding her into the opening act for their puppet show and tasking her with warming up the crowd as they traveled through the French countryside.*

*The harsh winter had been rough—her maman sick, her papa even worse. When they'd passed away, Colette had moved to Paris and learned how to get along on her own. Street performing brought in enough for food, some new clothes every now and then. When she'd met Francois, he'd taught her how to play to all sides of a group, not just back herself up against a wall, to maximize her crowd size.*

*The sun hadn't even risen yet as she tested out her tricks on the sidewalk, from a handstand to a somersault to a one-footed landing. Audience or no, Colette loved moving her body—feeling her muscles contract, her joints limber up.*

*Now if only Francois would arrive so they could run through more of their act. But he wasn't likely to show for another few hours. He didn't see the point—not until people were there to watch.*

*Mon dieu,* if only he understood practice is important. He is as sloppy as a dog chomping up food, *Colette thought.*

*She wondered how much longer she could keep him on as a partner. But then there were his forearms and how high he could throw her. Nothing thrilled her as much as being surrounded by air, the wind rushing past as though she were a bird.*

*As the streets began to fill, Colette decided a little solo performance to keep her warmed up wouldn't be such a bad idea. She set out a bucket, then waved to the passersby.*

*"Bonjour, ladies and gentlemen," she called. "If you will but give me a moment of your time, I hope to lighten your day with grace and skill."*

*Soon a space cleared around her and a small group gathered at the edges.*

*Bowing, she then flew into a series of backflips, her sewn-down-the-middle skirt safekeeping her modesty as she continued through her routine—or as much of it as she could do without Francois.*

*A handful of people dropped coins into the bucket, Colette's heart lifting with each clink. She nodded her thanks between moves, then noticed a set of piercing blue eyes staring at her. The man was handsome and his suit finely tailored, indicating money . . . lots of it. He was looking at her as though she were a painting, yet the intensity of his gaze unsettled her a bit.*

*She launched herself up into the air to catch hold of a flagpole outside the bakery. Swinging back and forth to get momentum, she finally let go and somersaulted through the air, boots clicking down solidly on the cement.*

*Yes! Colette loved it when the cheers were this genuine. She delicately picked up the bucket and shyly proffered it around the circle, garnering her some extra money before the crowd drifted away. Only the blue-eyed gentleman remained.*

*"Brava! You are incredible," he said, clapping as he approached. He sounded foreign—American, maybe?*

*"Merci, monsieur." Colette curtsied.*

*"My name is V. A. Vandevere."*

*"V. A.?" She'd heard of some high-profile businessmen*

*and politicians going by initials only; maybe they thought it made them seem more important somehow.*

*"Yes, and you are?"*

*"Colette Marchant."*

*"Colette, may I invite you to lunch?"*

*Colette hesitated, studying the man. He seemed harmless enough, and if it were a public restaurant then perhaps it would be okay.*

*"I assure you, I have the purest of intentions, although your beauty is quite striking. I own a fairground in New York City that we're developing into a park, and I'd love to talk to you about joining our team."*

*Over the man's shoulder, she spotted Francois finally arriving, his clothing disheveled. She raised an eyebrow at him.* You're too late.

*Francois seemed to understand her irritation. Shrugging, he turned away and wandered off. Colette would talk to him later, but first, she'd hear what this V. A. Vandevere had to say.*

# NEW JERSEY, 1917

How did I let V. A. talk me into this? *Colette wondered angrily as she stared at the control system in front of her. The airplane cockpit was ridiculously cramped; she could barely move her legs or arms.* When V. A. said he could make my dream of flying come true, this was not what I had in mind.

*"Okay," V. A. called through a megaphone. "We're ready to do another take. You all set, Colette?"*

*She turned her head to roll her eyes at him, but she couldn't see beyond the harsh lights of the film crew. Of course the pilot goggles encasing her eyes would have stopped him from seeing her annoyance in any case.*

*"Oui, I am ready. I am always ready," she replied testily. She'd been packed into this cockpit for an hour already as the crew moved the lights and backdrop and sound booms and cameras and then shuffled them all again until they wound up back in their original spots.*

*"On three, two, one—action!" V. A. chose to ignore her passive-aggressive remark. Fine; maybe she could talk to him about it over dinner. As long as he didn't have one of their potential new sponsors plopped between them, keeping talk light and upbeat . . . always upbeat.*

*Colette gripped the wheel and pretended the air around her was shaking the plane, curving her mouth into a daredevil smile as she steered through turbulent clouds. Of course, it wasn't real. She was as stationary as a sack of flour and only three feet off the ground of the studio lot.*

*"Cut!"*

*What now? There was supposed to be an explosion of smoke outside her window.*

*While the engineers huddled in a corner, examining the combustion machine, she fiddled with her helmet, wishing she could just take it off.*

*"How are you doing, my pet?" V. A. asked. He was standing on the wing of the plane, eyes dancing.*

*A pet? Yes, she was a pet for him now, wasn't she? Performing tricks as needed, unquestioned loyalty expected. This was not what she had pictured when she had agreed to go into business with him, following him across the ocean to America.*

*"V. A., when will we be done with this?" Colette asked.*

*"We'll be wrapping in an hour."*

*She'd meant the film, not the day. But based off her former moviemaking experiences—she had three under her belt already as V. A. expanded his empire, spinning her into a star across stage and screen—*Dames Who Dared *still had at least another month of on-set time. Followed by another three months of V. A.'s editing team poring over film.*

*Colette sighed. The movies were fun to see in the theater and she appreciated that they were the shiny future of entertainment, but everything moved so slowly in film. Sustaining her energy without an audience to feed off, unable to stretch and soar, not getting to do the type of performing she excelled at—it was draining.*

*All the drama was meant to come from within, to be conveyed with a tortured smile as the cameras zoomed in tighter and tighter, mere inches from her face. Colette preferred using her whole body—gracefully extending her arms and channeling the power of her legs to leap and balance.*

*"Am I performing at Dreamland next week?"*

*V. A. cocked his head, reading her mood. "If that's what your heart desires, then it shall be so. We can use the time to reshoot Bobby's scenes. Between you and me, he's so flat, I can hardly get a spark out of him."*

*Colette agreed. Her lackluster costar was yet another reason she found this particular movie so trying to work on.*

*"Thank you, V. A. I would like that."*

*Ever the gracious gentleman—as long as it suited his needs—V. A. nodded. "All right. I better go check on those pyromaniacs, make sure they're not overdoing the powder."*

*Colette watched him saunter away, then closed her eyes and leaned back in the hard leather seat. Soon she would be back in the air, dancing with the ribbon, twirling on a rope. Soon she'd be back at Dreamland. Soon.*

# CHAPTER
# THIRTEEN

rom a few stalls away, Holt could see Dumbo pop to his feet, hay slipping all around him as Holt and his kids approached. The little elephant must have heard them coming.

Milly and Joe burst through the swinging wooden doors into Dumbo's new pen with big smiles on their faces.

"Dumbo," they cried, flinging their arms around him. He poked his trunk at their faces and sides, clearly delighted to see them. Holt scanned the pen, making sure Dumbo had food and plenty of water—he knew how much elephants consumed—but Vandevere's lot had taken good care of the new star. Holt turned to Skellig to shake his hand, but the other man was already addressing two burly guards who'd been posted outside the training tent.

"Captain Farrier is now in charge. No one sees the animal without his approval," Skellig said.

"It's Holt—just call me Holt."

"I thought you were a military man," Skellig drawled. "I also like to hunt. But not people. Too slow." He bared his teeth in a grin.

Holt studied Skellig. His mouth might have been smiling, but there was a glint in his eyes that made Holt think Skellig was only half joking. "Nice boots you bagged there. Sharkskin?"

"No. So you better keep your elephant on my good side, eh?" Skellig winked and sauntered away.

Holt hoped he would leave Dumbo alone. Skellig left a bad taste in his mouth—like soured cheese. Any man who took that much pleasure in the hunt couldn't respect animals the way Holt did.

Making his way to where his kids were embracing Dumbo, Holt leaned down and patted the elephant's head. "Hiya, Dumbo."

Dumbo's trunk circled around Holt's fake arm.

"Okay, Dumbo, do you mind?" Holt wriggled, but the elephant tugged anyway, pulling the arm off and twisting it into a pretzel. Milly and Joe cracked up.

"Can I get my arm back?" Holt reached for it as the elephant waved it in the air.

"And these are the hands I'll be putting my life in," Colette said dryly from the doorway of the tent.

Startled, Dumbo dropped the arm. Holt hurried to reattach it and brush as much of the hay off it as possible. *First I nearly toss elephant dung on her and now it looks like I can't control Dumbo.* Holt grimaced, wishing he could rewind and start again, but the famous acrobat and actress was already there. *May as well get started.*

Colette didn't seem to be wearing makeup and had on a simple black leotard. Surprisingly, her hair was short—she must have worn a wig most of the time. Her natural hair color suited her better, Holt thought. Shaking his head, he sized her up. She was petite, but muscled. Dumbo would have no trouble lifting her—it was whether his ears could hold them both in the air that worried Holt.

"Right. Welcome. For the record, this was not my idea, okay?" Holt led Dumbo out onto the main floor of the tent, which was scattered with equipment. Once in the middle, he attempted to cross his arms, but ended up awkwardly hugging himself with just the one. "Dumbo works alone."

"So do I." Colette tossed her head, then turned to

the others. "Bonjour, Milly, Joe . . . and you." Warily, she crouched down in front of Dumbo.

Dumbo edged back, but Milly and Joe prodded him toward her. He spun to face them instead, leaving his tail spinning inches from Colette's face.

Colette stood up quickly. "Charming."

*Better take charge here,* Holt thought. "Probably doesn't recognize you without your makeup."

"You speak for the elephant?" Colette said. Her eyebrow arched in challenge.

"Like Vandevere speaks for you," Holt countered.

Colette turned away and began stretching, ignoring him completely.

"Look, if I gotta teach you to fly—"

"Oh, I know how to fly," she interrupted. "Ever since I was a child. And *they* taught Dumbo to fly, no?" She gestured toward the kids, who elbowed each other in pride. Colette arched an eyebrow at Holt. "So I don't need your expertise."

Holt bristled. "Just so you know, I've been to France. It wasn't a good experience." Shaking his head, he stepped back and waved at her and the kids to continue. If she wanted them to teach her, so be it. He'd stand by and jump in when things fell apart.

\* \* \*

Focusing on the kids, Colette relaxed. She hated when people looked down on her skills. Maybe he thought she was just a pretty face. He'd never seen her perform; how could he assume she was some beginner? And he clearly thought his precious elephant would be blighted by her presence.

True, it was endearing how he'd accidentally rubbed hay into his hair as he scratched his head, and he was sweet with Dumbo. Nevertheless, she was more comfortable with Milly and Joe.

She crouched next to the kids and whispered conspiratorially, "Show me your secret! How on earth does your elephant fly?"

"Well, first he needs his feather," Milly said.

"He won't fly without a feather." Joe shook his head emphatically. He bent and opened up a satchel.

Colette peered inside. It was stuffed to the brim with fluffy white feathers, the kind that poked out of mattresses and pillows. She peered at the kids again. They weren't joking.

"Well, then," she said, "neither will I."

Not knowing what to expect, Colette picked up some feathers and held them out to Dumbo. He sniffed them curiously and she backed away, leading him over to a bench with a teeterboard next to it. Once he was on the bench, she stood on the board, tipping it up toward the bench. She tossed the feather into the air. Focused on catching it, Dumbo didn't notice that he was stepping out until his foot came down on the board, launching Colette off the other end.

Milly and Joe gasped as the aerialist flung out her arm and expertly caught a ring hanging from a rope. She wove her hands and legs through the lyra and arched her back like the prow of a ship.

"Whoa, slow down there, princess," Holt called. "Safety first. Guys, get the nets." He waved at the guards to come help.

Colette smiled at Dumbo and waved as the nets were raised.

"See, Dumbo?" she called. "I fly just like you!" She twirled, her body weaving in and out of the lyra as though it were a dance partner. Dumbo's eyes followed her, his head cocked to the side. "Now let's see if you can catch me."

Colette dangled a feather above Dumbo. With a quick happy trumpet, Dumbo trotted over to Joe's bag and sucked up a handful of feathers. His ears flared and flapped . . . and, with one big push-off, he flew *up, up, up*.

*"Mon dieu,"* Colette whispered. She hadn't believed until this moment that it was really possible. But there he was, circling the tent until he was ten feet off the

ground, eyes wide with excitement . . . and headed straight for her.

"*Arrêtez*, elephant! *Arrêtez!*" Colette begged him to stop and flung the feather away.

Dumbo's ears flared out to brake, but he crashed into the side of the lyra, sending it and her into a wild swing. Colette shrieked as she lost her grip, hanging only by one leg from the ring. Below her, the ground swooped past as the lyra's momentum carried it back and it smacked into Dumbo from behind.

"*Eeeeuuuggh!*" Dumbo trumpeted in surprise. He flapped forward, but his tail was caught in the hook connecting the ring to the rope. Panicking, he tried to escape the strange thing tangled in his tail, his ears pushing him higher and twisting his body this way and that.

"*Aaaaaah!*" Colette screamed as Dumbo's frantic movements tore the lyra out of her grasp, and she plummeted toward the ground.

Finally free of the ring, Dumbo froze. He exhaled the feathers and, not flapping, cannoned down.

*Fwwooop.* Colette landed in a net and closed her eyes in relief.

"Look out!" Milly cried.

Eyes snapping open, Colette saw a ball of gray headed straight for her. She rolled to the side just as

Dumbo hit the net, dipping it so far down that she slid back into him.

A feather drifted down onto Colette's head. Smiling, Dumbo stuck his trunk out and *thwoooped* it up.

"We got some work to do," Holt's gruff voice proclaimed.

Colette struggled free of Dumbo's legs and flipped over the edge of the net, landing gracefully on the ground. Getting Dumbo down was a whole other spectacle, but the kids and roustabouts helped. Once he was back safely on the ground, Colette rubbed his head.

They had some practicing to do, but the little elephant had won her heart. He truly was something unexpected. And something special.

# CHAPTER
# FOURTEEN

*This is really happening.* Medici surreptitiously pinched himself through the pocket of his best coat. Though it was a bold checkered pattern, it looked shoddy next to Vandevere's smooth, simple striped jacket. *You can do this,* Medici told himself as Sotheby held the door open for them. Medici puffed out his chest. It wasn't the clothes that made the man, it was *how* the man wore them—no different from a costume in the ring. So he would wear *his* with confidence.

Medici strolled into the headquarters of Dreamland like he owned the place. Which—technically—he supposed he did. Partly.

Half a dozen desks were arranged inside, with frosted-glass doors leading into unknown chambers. The women and men at the desks rose to their feet as Vandevere followed him in. They eyed Medici with curiosity.

Sotheby stepped forward and cleared his throat. "Friends and colleagues, let's give a warm Dreamland welcome to our new executive vice president, Mr. Max Medici. Anything he needs, anything at all, make it happen as you always do."

The assistants clapped their hands and smiled as Sotheby led Medici through the desks to one of the doors. Swinging it open, he revealed Medici's new office.

Medici's jaw nearly dropped. The outer wall was floor-to-ceiling glass, giving him a clear view of the amusement park below. An enormous leather chair waited behind a cherrywood desk. Medici forced himself to walk—not run—to the chair and slid into it. The cushion was soft, but the arms of the chair were a tad high for him. No matter.

In the corner, a second desk and chair was occupied by a gray-haired woman with a pinched mouth. She seemed decidedly less friendly than any of the workers in the central room.

Sotheby gestured to her. "Miss Verna will handle your schedule, your correspondence, and all your calls.

When you're needed in meetings, she'll let you know."

Medici beamed at her, and she glared back. Maybe she just needed time to warm up to him. "Are there meetings today?" he asked brightly.

"I'll let you know," Verna snapped. Her fingers slammed down on the keys of the typewriter.

Vandevere nodded curtly to Medici from the doorway, then turned to go to his own office, Sotheby trailing behind.

"Mr. Vandevere, one question!" Medici called, half rising from his chair. But the other men were gone, leaving him with the steely-eyed Verna. He plopped back into his seat. "What exactly do I do?" he wondered.

* * *

After hours of practicing—with breaks to let Dumbo rest and give him well-earned rubdowns—Holt sat mending a net, using his teeth as a counterweight for knots, while Milly and Joe rewarded Dumbo with a bucket of peanuts. Across the tent, Colette did backflips and handstands on the teeterboard, keeping her muscles warmed up for the next session. Holt studied her. Her face relaxed as she spun through her moves, seeming to truly enjoy it. Everything around her appeared to drop away, like it was just her, the board, and the air, all in balance. It wasn't what he'd expected from Vandevere's starlet.

"Where'd Vandevere find you?" Holt asked.

"I was a street performer in Paris," Colette explained. "And he discovered me. And here I am." She shrugged at Holt's bemused stare.

"Millionaire's girlfriend. Real tough break," he joked.

"Oh, it's all for show." Holt's eyes widened in surprise. Colette must have noticed, because she continued, "He's got me acting in his pictures now, trying to launch his movie studio. But I can't stand it. It's the circus that I love." She leapt off the board and grabbed hold of a rope, swinging her body out to the side, the rushing air tickling her face.

"You two—you're not—together?" Holt silently cursed how awkward he sounded. It was none of his business. And yet he still sort of cared about the answer.

Colette's gaze was fixed on her hand as she slowly curled it through the air. "I'm one of many gems he wears to reflect light back onto him," she said. Her voice was sad and tinged with self-recrimination. But what did she have to be sorry about?

She slowed the rope and eased back to the ground, her eyes drifting to where Milly and Joe guided Dumbo through a warm-up using the triangular flags they'd made.

"I think *you* are the lucky one," she said.

Holt followed her gaze. Milly pointed the flags to both sides, directing Dumbo to flare his ears. Joe clapped and threw Dumbo a peanut when the elephant got the move right.

"Who's been dreaming like I've been dreaming?" a voice called, the words thrumming in the space.

Vandevere stood framed in the tent's entrance, his eyebrow arched with anticipation.

The net slid off Holt's lap as he stood and tipped his hat to his new boss. "We're making progress, but he's not quite ready."

* * *

*Not quite ready?* Vandevere's good mood burst. He eyed Holt, who'd been ogling Colette just a minute ago. If he had time for that, surely he had time to train Dumbo. That was his job, after all.

"What's wrong?" Vandevere growled. "Doesn't the animal trust you?"

"It's not that simple," Colette interjected. "It's about balance and weight—"

With a tight smile, Vandevere turned to her. So now she was defending the newbie?

"*Cherie*, the tickets have been sold." The act had to work—in four nights' time, the tent would be packed, Vandevere's future hanging in the balance. "Where's my little scientist?" He crossed to Milly and crouched down, looking straight into her eyes. "Why don't you show me that it's going to work?"

Milly darted a nervous glance at her dad, but he nodded. Straightening her back, she spun to Joe as Vandevere stood back to give them room. "Attention on the runway," she called.

Joe tripped on his way to take his place, quickly scrambling to his feet and dusting off his pants as he rose. Vandevere's lips pinched together, impatient for them to get on with it.

Once in front of Dumbo, Joe tucked the flags in to his sides. "Prepare for takeoff," he told Dumbo as he faced him.

"Flight test—left wing!" Milly commanded. Joe snapped a flag to his right and Dumbo's left ear unfurled and wagged in the air.

"Check," Joe called back to Milly.

"Right wing," Milly prompted.

"Check," Joe said as Dumbo responded to Joe's next flag move smoothly.

"And rudder."

Joe grinned as he spun a flag around his wrist

and Dumbo twirled his tail in answer. "Check!"

Next to Colette, Vandevere raised his eyebrow at her. Was this what they'd spent all day on?

"Oh, V. A.," Colette whispered, "let the kids have their fun."

Suddenly, Joe whirled and pointed both flags at Colette.

"Take her up, Dumbo!" Milly called. She whispered something in the elephant's large ear, too softly for Vandevere to catch, though he thought he heard the word *mom*.

Wriggling in delight, Dumbo snorted up the nearest feather and bounded toward the adults, his footfalls thundering. As the elephant neared, Vandevere scrambled out of the way, tripping over the net Holt had been mending.

Dumbo lowered his head, but he was moving too fast and his trunk didn't get a clear hold on Colette. She flipped through the air over his back and only just managed to land on her feet on the board.

"You really must wait till I'm ready," she said as Dumbo pivoted and galloped back again.

"Dumbo, settle down," Milly pleaded as he charged into Colette.

Again, his momentum was too much, and his trunk knocked her legs into the air. From the ground,

Vandevere glowered. This was what he'd partnered with Medici for? A clumsy, galloping elephant bound to the ground?

But then Colette caught hold of Dumbo's ear. She swung herself into position on his back, her legs and arms wrapped around him.

Dumbo's ears flapped. The wind from his movement forced Vandevere to squint. Together, Dumbo and Colette lifted into the air, climbing higher as he circled the tent.

Vandevere's heart skipped a beat.

The elephant *could* fly.

"Woo-hoo! Higher, Dumbo," Milly and Joe called.

Vandevere let Holt help him up from the ground; he was too busy staring at the impossible coming true.

Astride the flying elephant—the honest-to-goodness *flying* elephant—Colette sat up and reached out her arms, brushing the top of the tent. Tingles ran down Vandevere's skin and laughter bubbled up from his chest.

Hugging Holt to him, Vandevere beamed. "You beautiful, crippled cowboy. You just made me a child again."

The men stood together watching Dumbo and Colette zoom through the air. Milly and Joe whooped and hollered. The air fizzled with magic. Dreams really could come true.

# PUCK
## DREAMLAND,
## NEW YORK, 1920

*The cot squeaked underneath Puck as he shifted his weight, leaning over to grab his guitar. The tents Vandevere had put most of the Medici performers in (the Farriers' link to Dumbo elevated them) were much nicer than their old ones. The fabric was thick enough to protect against winter winds, but there were screened sections that could be opened in the summer. Quite ingenious.*

*And yet, it was too quiet back in this section of the park, sequestered away from the bustle of the main fairgrounds. They weren't even anywhere near Dreamland's performers, whose housing was rumored to be brick-and-mortar.*

*The tents were nicer and the mattresses fluffier, but he missed the cozy camaraderie of their old setup. Reluctantly he admitted to himself that he even missed the campfire cookouts. Here food was served in a dining hall with people slopping stew onto their plates and then scattering across tables and benches. More civilized than the cobbled-together stools and chairs and logs of the* traveling circus, sure, but no one really talked to anyone else. They just shoveled their food in and left.

The food was bland, too. Rongo had assured him he liked Puck's better.

Strumming his guitar, Puck hummed softly.

"Can I join you?" a sweet voice asked from outside.

Puck bolted upright, then quickly scanned his tent. "Um, um." He kicked his dirty socks under the bed and swept the pages of a script he'd been writing off the chair and onto a side table instead. "Of course. Please come in."

Miss Atlantis ducked into the tent, a pile of books in her hands.

Puck's eyes widened. "Where did you get those?" he blurted. Then he blushed. He should have at least said hello first.

She didn't seem to notice his slip in etiquette, or mind it if she did.

"Milly brought them to me. Apparently there's a whole library in the house where they're staying. She wanted us to share them, knowing how much we both love to read." Miss Atlantis smiled tentatively, then handed over the top three to Puck.

Twelfth Night and The Tempest by Shakespeare, which he couldn't wait to reread, and a new one, The Magic of Oz by Frank L. Baum. He'd heard of this series of adventures in a far-off land.

*"I thought we could, if you'd like, read them and then discuss them afterwards?" she said.*

*He looked up from his pile. Her face was earnest, open, and nervous. Maybe she was just as anxious around him as he was around her.*

*"That'd be—that'd be great," he answered. This was his chance! He could prove to her how deep his thoughts went, how vast his emotional scope and empathy. Maybe they could do dramatic readings and his voice would roll out, weaving a spell over her heart the way her voice had done to his when they'd first met.*

*"Wonderful. It's settled, then." She glanced around the tent, and his gaze followed hers. "It's a bit dark in here for reading at the moment, though. Perhaps we could take a walk through the fairgrounds?"*

*Puck nodded, having lost control of his voice. So much for weaving a spell over her. "Um, uh, yes, um, I mean"—he coughed—"I'd be delighted."*

*As they meandered through the makeshift tent city of Medici's troupe, Puck darted glances at Miss Atlantis. He had to keep reassuring himself this was happening. Subtly, he steered her toward Rongo's tent. Maybe a witness would help him confirm later it hadn't all been a dream.*

*In front of his tent, the strongman hefted a set of weights up to his shoulders and pressed it upward, his muscles straining.*

"Rongo!" Puck called in greeting.

Rongo held the weight a moment longer, then dropped it and stepped back so it wouldn't crush his feet. A wide grin broke over his face when he saw Puck and Miss Atlantis approaching.

"Good evening," Rongo said.

"Hello, Rongo," Miss Atlantis said. "So you're practicing, too? I saw Catherine and Ivan on my way over to Puck's tent and they were huddled over some new device. Wouldn't let me closer, of course, saying they need to preserve the mystery or something." She shrugged, a smile on her lips to show she didn't mind.

"Yes," Rongo answered. "I wanted to be ready for when we go on. Should be any day now, eh? Wonder what's taking Max so long to get us scheduled." Rongo swung his arms back and forth, cracking his shoulders.

"Max is doing his best, I'm sure. You know he will take care of us. He's never let us down before. The logistics must be complicated," Puck said.

He had faith in Medici. The circus director could be grouchy at times, but even when he was bellowing orders, everyone felt the undercurrent of care Medici felt for them. He loved his circus, he loved his troupe, and he'd make sure they had a place onstage.

"What if Vandevere is the one holding it up?" Miss

Atlantis asked, her eyes worried. "What if he wants us to audition for him first?"

"I'll be ready no matter what he wants," Rongo said. He waved toward an array of weights and objects behind him.

A pang of anxiety struck Puck's stomach, and he felt his hands get clammy. "Audition?" What if he finally got to perform his monologues? But then again, what if he wasn't good enough? Most of the time, he felt the audience was more focused on Barrymore than him. What if he couldn't hold his own without the monkey? Vandevere might want to separate them.

Rongo patted Puck on the shoulder. "You will do fine, Puck." He glanced at Miss Atlantis. "But perhaps Miss Atlantis could listen to your Shakespeare act, give you some feedback?"

"Of course, I'd be happy to!" Miss Atlantis clapped her hands and beamed.

"Really, you wouldn't mind?" Puck tugged nervously on his shirt.

"I'd be delighted," she answered. "Come on, let's go find a suitable rehearsal space."

Twenty minutes later they were settled in a training tent. Miss Atlantis had rounded up a few of the clowns and acrobats, as well as Catherine and Ivan, insisting *they would have great advice about stage presence. Rongo had demurred, wanting to finish his workout, and Pramesh and Arav had been busy feeding their snakes, so Miss Atlantis and Puck had hastily left them to it.*

*Puck strode to the center of the ring, then closed his eyes and widened his stance. Breathing deeply, he shed his anxieties and fears, drawing from his core, settling the mantle of his character around him.*

*He was self-taught aside from a smattering of lessons in elocution, but ever since he was a child he'd been able to imitate any sound or phrase he heard. His parents used to laugh and laugh whenever he copied one of them or, even better, their nosy neighbors.*

*All around him, the people he met fed into the characters he created onstage.*

*His shoulders relaxed and his body shifted, confidence spreading through him. When he opened his eyes he was* the *Puck—the character who had lent him his stage name, the trickster mischief-maker of* A Midsummer Night's Dream, *ready to lead another astray.*

*"'What hempen homespuns have we swaggering here, so near the cradle of the fairy queen?'" Puck mimed finding a group of humans close by, his expression affronted. Then a gleam came to his eye.*

*He winked at the audience then crouched as though hiding behind a tree. "I'll follow you. I'll lead you* about a round, through bog, through bush, through brake, through brier. Sometime a horse I'll be, sometime a hound, a hog, a headless bear, sometime a fire. And neigh, and bark, and grunt, and roar, and burn, like horse, hound, hog, bear, fire, at every turn.'"

With each animal he listed, he vocalized their sound, neighing and snorting and roaring ferociously. The troupe members cheered at each, but when he got to his imitation of the crackling of a fire, a gasp of silence met him.

Fearing the worst, Puck peered up at them, his eyes searching out Miss Atlantis.

Surprise lit her face. She squealed and rose to her feet, clapping madly.

"Bravo, Puck, bravo! How did you do that?" she cried.

"It sounded like a real fire," Ivan marveled. "Could you work that into your show?"

"Not to mention the bear." Catherine gave a little shudder. "Too realistic for me."

"Eh! That was the best part," Spiros boomed.

"More, please," Miss Atlantis called.

Beaming, Puck bowed graciously, like a courtier. "Whatever my lady wishes."

"What else can you do?" Ivan asked.

"How about a lion?" Demosthenes, another clown, suggested.

"Or a snake," Lulu the acrobat said.

"No, I know," Miss Atlantis broke in, her smile wide. "The best animal of all. An elephant."

The group whooped in agreement.

Shaking his shoulders loose, Puck slumped over, letting one front arm dangle like a trunk, the other imitating a front leg. He shuffled along the ground, then pretended to spot danger.

Rearing up, he lifted his "trunk" high and bellowed like he'd heard Mrs. Jumbo do back in Joplin.

An answering "Eeeeuugh!" startled the group. They turned to see Dumbo in the doorway, Holt and the kids at his side.

"Dumbo!" Miss Atlantis called.

"Welcome!" Puck waved hello.

"We came to investigate the ruckus," Holt said as they entered. Dumbo trotted over and nuzzled Puck, his trunk gently poking the actor in his side as though trying to tickle him.

"Yeah, it sounded like there was a full zoo in here," Joe said.

"And another elephant, so of course Dumbo charged away." Milly smiled at everyone.

Catherine and Ivan came down to the ring, giving both kids quick hugs before patting Dumbo.

"No, no elephant. Just me, sad to say." Puck lifted his shoulders in apology.

"Not 'just' you. That was amazing!" Miss Atlantis stood next to him, resting her hand on his arm. "You fooled Dumbo, after all!"

"I did, didn't I?" Puck's chest swelled with pride. He might not be a star act, but he could impersonate anyone and anything. Perhaps that could be worked into his act. If Barrymore was still to be part of his act, the monkey could even play off it, shrinking away from his lion, climbing his head after his elephant's call . . . Possibilities circled through his mind.

"You're all coming to the show tonight, right? For Dumbo's debut?" Joe asked.

"Of course," Puck said as everyone nodded. "We wouldn't miss it for the world."

He was eager to see Dreamland's main show with all its highlighted performers. None of them could top Dumbo; he was positive of that. It would be a fun evening, and it would give him a chance to figure out how to make his own act unique.

Just in case Vandevere did ask them all to audition—he'd be ready, with a bag of tricks all his own.

# CHAPTER
# FIFTEEN

olette and Dumbo waited backstage as Dreamland's biggest crowd yet filed into the main tent. A full orchestra, situated in its own fancy box above the floor, played the latest jazz hit.

Up in the VIP box, Vandevere gazed down at the masses below.

"The elephant's the turning point, Sotheby," he said. "They'll come from every corner of the globe for him." Who wouldn't want to see a genuine miracle?

"But, sir," Sotheby offered tentatively, "what if you're wrong?"

"I can't afford to be," Vandevere answered. He

smiled at his loyal aide and then moved into the gathering of the elite in the viewing box.

*"Buonasera!"* Medici boomed as he sauntered into the room. Only years of practicing a neutral expression kept Vandevere from recoiling at Medici's ill-fitting coat. At least it wasn't a tacky red or blue, but a sensible black. His new colleague oozed forward, shaking hands left and right. "Max Medici, I discovered the elephant. *Benvenuto*, the flying elephant is mine."

Vandevere shifted slightly, trying to block Medici from the view of the tall, elegant businessman he was courting. He needed J. Griffin Remington to approve his loan so he could pay off Dreamland's costs. Medici might turn Remington's stomach and ruin the deal.

"Aha, you're the guy," Remington said, looking over Vandevere's shoulder. "The man made out of lucky dust."

Hiding his annoyance, Vandevere turned and smiled. "Max, meet J. Griffin Remington of Atlas Forge Bank."

*"The* J—? Whoa, I'm honored." Medici swiped off his top hat.

"They say the moon is made of magic dust." Remington gestured skyward. "One day, we'll send a man there, you'll see. And Atlas Forge will finance the expedition. What do you think of that?"

"Needless to say, we all have high hopes for tonight," Vandevere said. Hopefully a *high* loan was in reach, as well.

"High hopes, yup," Max agreed.

"Hopes, dreams, they're words." Remington shrugged. "I prefer plans. Like V. A.'s here." He clapped Vandevere on the shoulder, beaming. "This guy's got plans. Going to take all the circuses in the country and meld them into one circus."

Medici blinked. "But I thought circuses were closing because of movies and radio."

"Trust me, Max, they are. We've just been helping things along," Vandevere said.

"But what's that take? A lot of money. Which he hasn't got." Remington turned to Vandevere, his face serious. "We're hoping that your pachyderm comes through with the goods." Brightening, he leaned down—far down—and planted a kiss on Medici's bald head. Vandevere relaxed—Remington had taken to Medici. "Because we want some of that magic dust!"

Laughing, Remington straightened, gave them both a half salute, and disappeared into the crowd.

Medici stared at his partner, the gears in his mind clearly turning.

*Better head off his questions now,* Vandevere thought. "The key to dealing with a bank is to let them think they're in control," he remarked aloud.

But Medici was not so easily distracted. "You've been buying *all* the circuses?" His voice was disapproving, almost accusatory.

Time to reel Medici in before he spun off. The best way to do that was to play on his loyalty, his need for family.

"Max, c'mon." Vandevere slapped him on the back. "Start saying 'we.' Come on, sit. Enjoy the show."

With that, Vandevere excused himself. Medici would enjoy the VIP view and rubbing elbows with the elite. He'd be singing the praises of Vandevere's plan in no time. Soon their circus would be the best—and only—one in the country, drawing thousands of visitors every month.

* * *

Medici bit his lip as Vandevere dove into the crowd, greeting other guests and oozing charm. What had that been about? Vandevere was buying out the competition, crushing circuses left and right? Had Medici been scammed? No, he was a partner now. His troupe was protected, guaranteed spots in Dreamland. They were in the center of it all now—the future of entertainment—and he intended to stay there.

Turning, Medici scanned the enormous auditorium

before him, where rows and rows of benches were filled with chattering people. The anticipation was palpable. His eyes found his troupe below—Rongo, Puck, Pramesh, Miss Atlantis, Ivan, and Catherine. They, too, seemed to wait with hope and big expectations. They were counting on him, just like Dumbo and the Farriers.

A steady drumroll—they must have had at least ten drums going at once!—boomed through the arena. Rongo cocked his head at the orchestra as if to say *There's no way one man alone could ever sound like* that. Medici shrugged. *You work with what you've got.*

Everyone hushed and settled in. Darkness descended as the lights were cut, but one bright spotlight clicked on, illuminating a dashing master of ceremonies.

Medici had met him a few days earlier—Baritone Bates, he was called. He had a chiseled chin and a habit of chewing toothpicks, but onstage he commanded the audience with just a twitch of his finger. Medici had to hand it to him—he had charisma, drawing everyone's eyes to him and holding their gaze, without even saying a word.

"Welcome," Bates finally intoned. "You've reached the only place on Earth where the impossible is possible: V. A. Vandevere's Dreamland Circus." His hands seemed to cup an imaginary flower and send it floating into the air. Opening his arms wide to invite people to lean in, he continued. "Rest your cares, set down your troubles, then close your eyes and follow me—into the land of all your dreams!"

Bates stepped backward with his last words, the spotlight trailing him, but all around the ring different areas lit up briefly.

*Ka-bang!* A quick flash showed a strongman lifting two women in the air—one balanced on each hand. *Whoosh.* Another light caught two acrobats swooping past on a trapeze. *Zing!* Up on a pedestal, a bare-chested man balanced the hilt of a sword on his forehead while juggling four more.

Each scene was polished and refined, from the shiny props to the flawless costumes to the disciplined performers. It gave a taste of the wonders to come. Dreamland clearly had a lot to offer.

Medici felt a twinge in his stomach. His troupe would have to step up their acts. But with adequate funds for costumes and props, and time to focus on rehearsals rather than help run the circus, he had confidence they could do it. They were just as good as anyone else there.

\* \* \*

Down below, his troupe was also sizing up the existing Dreamland acts. Puck shifted next to Rongo and leaned in. "I don't know. I guess I've seen worse," he grumbled.

Rongo harrumphed in agreement. He'd been working out and could easily lift those two women—maybe even one more if they stood on a board.

Miss Atlantis gasped as a group of dancers emerged on rolling platforms, stacked three rows high like a giant spinning cake. They kicked their legs in precise synchronization. On the floor below them, clowns balanced on top of large balls.

"They're good, huh?" she asked Pramesh.

He patted her hand reassuringly. "We all have our talents."

"They've got nothing on Dumbo," Puck declared.

"Ooh, I can't wait for him to come out!" Miss Atlantis clasped her hands in excitement.

* * *

Backstage, Holt, Milly, and Joe prepped Dumbo for the main act. Milly straightened the tasseled cape he was wearing. Joe pulled out an assortment of feathers, examining each one.

Holt leaned down and patted Dumbo, whose ears were swinging nervously. Holt followed the elephant's gaze to the ring and surrounding audience. The space seemed downright cavernous, a stark contrast to the warm, cozy backstage area they were in now. "Don't worry, Big D. Just more room to fly in there, that's all."

"Round and round, just like we practiced," Milly added. She shook a peanut bag. "All the peanuts you can eat when you get back."

"And then Dad can talk to Vandevere about the deal!" Joe piped up.

"About the what?" Holt asked.

"It's why he flies," Joe prattled on. "We made a deal with Dumbo, Dad. With all the money he makes for the circus, we promised him we'd buy back his mom." Joe's eyes shone and Dumbo nuzzled him with his trunk.

"You made a deal . . . with *Dumbo*?" Holt gazed back and forth between his kids.

Milly recognized the look on her dad's face—the disbelief, the shutting down. He was going to tell them it was impossible. And she didn't want Dumbo to hear that. "Joe, this isn't the time," she said.

"But we have to," her brother insisted. "Dad, we promised. If the circus won't do it, then you could—"

"I didn't make any deal." Holt shook his head, worry creasing his brow. He had no way of locating Dumbo's mother, even if Vandevere *would* part with the money for it. Nor was Holt getting paid, per se—they were earning room and board at the moment. Maybe once his own horse act was drawing in crowds, but he didn't know when that would be. . . . He couldn't bear to give his kids or the little elephant false hope. "Guys, truly, I'm sorry, but Mrs. Jumbo is gone."

Dumbo snorted and shook his head, backing away from Holt. His eyes brimmed with hurt.

"Shh, no, Dumbo. Don't listen to him," Milly said fiercely. They'd find a way; they had to.

Her dad sighed and knelt down next to her, setting his hand on her shoulder. "You can't make promises you can't keep, darlin'."

Milly's brown eyes were sharp as she met his gaze. "Like when you promised you'd come back?" Accusation wove through her words.

"I *did* come back," Holt said gently.

"You promised Mama." Milly's chin jutted into the air and she bit her lip to keep it from quivering.

Holt reeled backward as though she'd slapped him. Before he could think what to say, Colette bustled in, her silver leotard sparkling and a white feathered headpiece ringing her hair like a halo.

"*Bonne chance, mes amis!*" she called. "Are we ready?"

212

"Yeah, yeah, ready." Holt ducked his head, pretending to adjust Dumbo's halter to hide his face. "Are you?"

"Finale! Places!" The stage manager summoned them, but Colette stopped, her eyes on Milly's crumpled expression.

"Now, now, what's all this?" Colette glided over to her and crouched in front of her. "You know, in France, we kiss twice. For luck."

She pecked Milly once on each cheek, then did the same for Joe. Standing, Colette arched an eyebrow at Holt. Sheepishly, he shuffled forward and gave her a quick kiss on the cheek, then nearly bolted out of there, leading Dumbo along. Colette smiled to herself and rushed off to her own starting spot.

"Uh-oh," Joe said, gazing after them.

"What? What is it?" Milly asked.

"Dad only kissed her once." Joe's brow furrowed in worry. Together, the children peered through the curtain into the enormous Colosseum.

# CHAPTER
## SIXTEEN

arkness blanketed the space as Dumbo and Colette took their places. (Vandevere loved showmanship and had insisted they both appear as if from nowhere.) Suddenly, a pink glow appeared—dancers holding large rings paraded through the ring, trailed by giant bubbles that looked like ethereal elephants. A choir began singing about pink elephants hopping everywhere.

"Pink elephants?" Medici asked.

Remington smiled, though, clearly enjoying the absurdity.

"Ladies and gentlemen, boys and girls of all ages," Baritone Bates spoke from offstage. "And now, the moment you have been waiting for. V. A. Vandevere, in association with Max Medici, proudly presents, making his Dreamland debut, the one . . . the only . . . the legendary . . . Let's get ready for Dumbooooo!"

As he boomed out Dumbo's name, a spotlight clicked on in the center ring, where the elephant stood. Dumbo blinked in the brightness. Milly guessed he couldn't see anyone or anything beyond the spotlight, but he could at least hear the audience cheering and smell the popcorn and pretzels. The ground beneath him pushed up, lifting the pedestal just as they'd practiced. But it kept going—higher than she remembered. Nervously, Dumbo peered over the edge.

He was a hundred feet up. He'd flown at this height before, but he'd never taken off from someplace this high.

Milly clutched her key necklace. "He can do it. I know he can."

A drumroll sounded, and then, with a cymbal crash, a second light illuminated Colette, standing on the ground.

"And here to welcome him, our own immaculate Queen of the Heavens!" Baritone Bates exclaimed.

With a flourish, Colette plucked a feather from her headdress, then grabbed hold of a chandelier above her and began to run with it along the edge of the ring. Backstage, crew members cranked the chandelier higher, and Colette's feet lifted off the floor. She swung her body, arcing through the air, then wove her hands and feet through the branches, showing off some of her old act's impressive contortions.

The chandelier slowed as it circled Dumbo's pedestal and Colette delicately hung from it with one hand as her toes gently touched down next to him.

The audience cheered.

Colette waved to them as the chandelier was whisked away. Dumbo shifted uncomfortably on the small platform.

"Dumbo, it's me," Colette whispered. "Five times around the ring. That's all we have to do." Holding the feather aloft, she circled him and swung into the saddle on his back. "Nice and easy, like we practiced."

Dumbo wobbled, but quickly adjusted to her weight. *Whoosh*, his ears flared out sideways. A true performer, Colette flung her arms wide to match him, keeping a tight hold of the feather.

The audience burst into applause, but Milly grabbed hold of her dad's shirt. "Dad, the nets! Why aren't they putting up the nets?"

Holt followed her gaze. The stagehands who *should* have been raising the safety nets into place were instead lounging backstage. He hurried over to the stage manager.

"What's going on? Your men are supposed to be out there!"

The stage manager barely glanced at him. "Change of plan. From the tippy-top."

In the balcony section, Medici had also noticed the problem. He leaned over to Vandevere and whispered urgently, "I don't see the nets."

Vandevere's eyes were on Remington, who gave him an impressed nod. "They're invisible," Vandevere told Medici. Medici bit his lip, eyes still scanning for ropes in the darkness.

Turning back to the arena, Vandevere saw Colette's eyes on him, her shoulders tense. He tipped his hat to her. "No risk, no reward. She'll thank me later," he muttered. "When she is a legend and we are catapulted into the halls of fame together."

The crowd murmured, a low buzz of excitement and adrenaline, but they didn't know what was in store.

"Who's been dreaming like I've been dreaming?" Vandevere whispered.

Down below, Holt hissed in anger. "They need nets, what's wrong with you?" He stormed toward the net controls himself, calling up, "Colette, don't take off, wait!"

The stage manager and three stagehands converged on him, blocking his path. No matter which way he dodged, they stopped him. Holt charged at them, but he was outnumbered, and they wrestled him back.

"Eeeugh?" Dumbo let out a nervous trumpet, confused as to why Holt had suddenly appeared and then disappeared.

The pedestal wobbled under him. Colette took a deep breath, tightening her knees around his sides. Holding the feather aloft, she extended it in front of his face. Dumbo brightened and grasped it in his trunk.

"Dumbo!" Colette's voice rang out in the arena. "Prince of the Elephants, I command you to fly with me."

She clapped her hands, chalk dust puffing into the air and momentarily blinding Dumbo. Blinking rapidly, he sneezed, shooting the feather from his grasp.

"No!" Joe cried.

As Dumbo lunged for it, Colette was thrown forward. Frantic, she grabbed hold of Dumbo's cape and saddle, but both came with her as she flipped over Dumbo's head. Unable to see, Dumbo spun, trying to shift the cape. Colette's feet hung out over open space.

Milly's heart thumped wildly in her chest.

*Snap!* The belt of the saddle broke free.

"Aaah!" Clinging to just the cape, Colette dropped, but now that he could see again, Dumbo shot out his trunk and wrapped it around the other end of the cape. He leaned backward, using his weight to try to heft Colette back up onto the platform.

Snapping out of their horror, the stagehands rushed to unfurl the nets, letting Holt go as well. He hurried out to help.

"Fly, Dumbo, fly!" Holt called.

"He needs the feather," Milly said. She clutched Joe to her side, wondering if she should cover his eyes.

By now the stagehands had the net half unfurled, but it wouldn't be ready in time. Holt darted backstage.

*Riiiiip.* A tear formed in the twisted fabric of the cape.

Colette's eyes widened in fear and she locked gazes with Dumbo. "Please! Fly for *me*, fly for—"

*Riiiip-snap.* The cape split in two.

"Aaaaaaaaaahhhh!!!!" Colette's scream pierced the arena, and the audience echoed her cry.

Out of nowhere, a rope sailed toward her and she grabbed hold of it. Hooked around a peg, the rope swung her, slowing her descent until she slid into the arm of the rope-wielder, knocking them both to the ground. Holt. The cowboy had saved her.

On the pedestal, Dumbo was in trouble. The recoil from the cape's splitting had sent his hind legs sliding off the platform and now he scrambled to stay on, pushing his trunk and ears flat to the wood as if embracing it and clamping down on the edge with his mouth.

*"EEEEEEEEEEEUUUUUUUGH!!!"* Dumbo shrieked.

"Lower the platform!" Holt boomed, pushing himself to standing.

Dumbo trumpeted again, terrified.

\* \* \*

The sad sound carried, washing over the audience and then beyond. It flew over the fairgrounds, past the Ferris wheel and roller coasters, and across a makeshift moat to the spooky attraction of Nightmare Island.

There, Dumbo's cry traveled down the corridor of caged predators—from the snarling lion, to the bored grizzly bear, to the patient crocodile—to the very last cage, where a pair of ears swiveled in concern. A sign outside read KALI THE DESTROYER, KILLER OF MEN. The elephant within was decked out in chains, some decorative, some real, along with a bold red head scarf and a blanket trimmed in golden tassels. Paint ringed her eyes, making them look fierce, and more dabbles

of color flared out along her trunk, almost like miniature flames. Rising up on her hind legs, the elephant
roared an answering bellow—reverberating through
the very ground as it bounced back to Dumbo.

* * *

Back at the Colosseum, Dumbo recognized the sound
instantly. It was *her*! Reenergized, Dumbo perked up
his ears, but without their help to cling to the platform, he slipped farther. Then his eyes landed on a
few errant feathers from Colette's headpiece.

*Fwwwoop*. Dumbo suctioned them up as he tumbled backward, gravity pulling him down.

The audience gasped and Vandevere tensed.

"Nooo!" Medici cried.

Milly forced Joe to turn away with her. She couldn't
bear to watch.

Then she heard the crowd cheer. Tentatively, she
turned.

There was Dumbo zooming upward, his ears flapping, a smile on his face.

"He's okay!" Milly hugged Joe as they both jumped
up and down in relief.

Colette flung her arms around Holt, startling him
as celebrations broke out among the crew and Medici's
troupe. The audience, now believing it had all been

part of the act, clapped wildly. Up in the VIP section, Remington and his banker friends toasted one other, and Vandevere relaxed. His eyes followed the elephant. Then he turned his gaze to watch the crowd experience it for the first time.

Dumbo trumpeted loudly and flattened his ears like a plane's wings, angling toward an exit. People screeched and ducked as he whooshed overhead, his feet mere inches from their hair. Tilting sideways, Dumbo slipped out of the tent and burst into the main fairgrounds.

"What the—?" a balloon man cried as the elephant barreled into his wares, popping several at once.

Dumbo somersaulted and plopped face-first into the dirt. He quickly jumped to his feet, trumpeting again.

*There!* In the distance he heard his mama respond. Without hesitation, Dumbo launched himself into the air. Nothing could keep him from her now.

From above, people looked so tiny, but as Dumbo dove toward his destination, he had to swerve to avoid hitting anyone. The creepy structure in front of him looked like a volcano with a skull carved into it— the gaping, toothed mouth the entrance. The skull's eyes were lit from within, flickering ominously. It did not look inviting. But he could hear his mother inside. Without slowing down, Dumbo swooped over the moat, past the bridge, and right through the mouth.

Mrs. Jumbo—now known as Kali—trumpeted in joy as her son galloped toward her across the stone floor. They'd found each other!

*Thump.* Dumbo slammed against the bars of her cage. The two elephants stretched their trunks as close as they could, but Mrs. Jumbo's chains kept her back. Try as he might, all Dumbo could feel was the hard, cold surface of the bars pressing into his skin, keeping him and his mother apart.

\* \* \*

In the VIP box, Vandevere whirled on Medici, his face red. "Where'd he go? Where's my show? Get out and GET MY ELEPHANT BACK!" he roared.

Medici bolted, finding Holt, Milly, Joe, and Colette outside. They pointed skyward, tracing the path Dumbo had taken through the air.

Milly couldn't understand. He'd never done anything like this. What could have gotten into him? Where was he going? There was only one way to find out. They took off after him.

Up ahead, they saw a scary cave, surrounded by a moat. Torches illuminated an oily slick on the water below the wooden bridge. Signs out front identified it as Nightmare Island. Why would Dumbo come here?

Milly and Joe sped up, with Holt and Colette close behind.

"Dumbo, it's all right!" Milly called.

"We're here," Joe yelled as they tumbled into the stone structure.

Then they spotted them: Dumbo standing in front of a larger elephant within a caged enclosure. The larger elephant reared back, bellowing, but Dumbo seemed oblivious to the humans.

Milly and Joe heard footsteps behind them and suddenly Skellig and some guards charged past. Dumbo didn't register the danger until it was too late. Thick ropes cinched around him as Skellig and his men caught him in their net.

Dumbo tossed his head, crying out.

Vandevere stormed in, his usually perfect hair askew. Hot on his heels, Medici glanced up at his new partner and grinned when he saw Vandevere wore a toupee.

A group of teenagers gawked at them from in front of the lion's cage. Seeing they were not alone, Vandevere plastered on a fake smile and clapped.

"Hi, how are you? Having fun?" he said. Reaching

Skellig, he lowered his voice. "Hurry up and get him out of here."

As the men lugged Dumbo away from the larger elephant, Dumbo struggled, flinging his ears and legs wide.

"Guys, he's a baby. Go easy—gentle!" Holt said.

Skellig shoved past him, tugging on the net. "Soldier, I give the orders here."

Joe turned away, studying the strange collection of creatures. Milly followed him to the elephant's cage.

"He heard her. He flew here . . . to her." She wondered what about this elephant would summon Dumbo. He never acted that way around Zeppelin or Goliath. Was it because she was female? Milly knew elephant herds were led by a matriarch.

"Milly, look!" Joe's words brought her back to her surroundings. "That face, those eyes."

Milly peered in through the bars. If you took away the paint around her eyes and along her trunk, stripped away the golden harness . . .

"Dad!" Milly raced to where her dad stood with Colette. "It's Mrs. Jumbo! She's *here*. Dumbo's mom is RIGHT HERE!" She pulled him down the aisle to see for himself.

Mrs. Jumbo paced anxiously in her cage, her trunk

swaying along the ground. That was her, all right. It was clear in the way she moved, in the markings on her skin. As his kids whooped and danced, Holt studied the plaque in front of the cage.

KALI THE DESTROYER, KILLER OF MEN: SHE HATH SLAUGHTERED INNOCENT SOULS AT MANY CIRCUSES! GAZE UPON HER IF YOU DARE! A FEARSOME BEAST WHOSE VENGEANCE CANNOT BE TAMED!

Holt winced, his heart twisting with worry. Yes, they'd found Dumbo's mom. Yes, she was already at Dreamland. But somehow, Holt didn't think they were going to get the happy reunion his kids hoped for.

# CHAPTER
## SEVENTEEN

andevere hustled back to the Colosseum. He normally hated to move above a saunter, and this was the second time tonight he had been rushed. But Remington and his money hung on the line.

Sure enough, as he rounded the path to the Colosseum, he spotted the banker and his associates stepping into their cars. That wouldn't do. Not at all. Ignoring the huffing and puffing of Medici behind him and the calls for refunds from the people streaming out of the Colosseum, Vandevere lengthened his stride to reach the vehicles.

"J.G.R., wait," he called. "What's the problem?

The elephant flies! You *saw* it." It was impossible for Remington to deny or ignore.

"Yeah, I got eyes," Remington drawled. "I saw a vanishing act. Kiddies crying to their mommies, people yelling for their money back. You can't control your animal."

Vandevere stepped up onto the sideboard of the car, hand outstretched. "Give me some time. I can fix it." His tone was even, but his heart fluttered in his chest.

Remington narrowed his eyes, then pulled the door shut and sat down. "Bank's closed until you can." He waved to the driver, and Vandevere leapt off as the motor revved.

Dust covered his shoes as the cars peeled out, one after the other. He wouldn't let his dreams be taken away. He'd worked too hard to get to where he was to let a sloppy trainer and mishandled animal drag him down.

"V. A." Medici panted as he caught up. "What's going on?"

"Precisely what I'm going to find out." Vandevere gritted his teeth and stormed toward his office. Medici, like a lapdog, skittered after him.

Up at the top of the tower, Colette whirled toward them as the elevator doors pinged open. Her eyes sparked in fury, but Vandevere's matched hers.

"What happened up there?" he snapped. "You lost control of your animal."

"You're the animal!" Colette fumed. "Where was my net?" Even through her makeup, her cheeks were flushed pink. "I nearly died."

Vandevere didn't see it that way. "Nets are for rehearsal. This is the show." If she wasn't going to step up, he'd find another star to ride Dumbo. He spotted the silhouette of Holt inside his office. Flinging open the door, Vandevere startled Holt and his kids.

"Training? You call that training?" Vandevere could feel a blood vessel pulsing in his forehead. He'd need a long hot bath to unwind from tonight.

"Hold on, Mr. Vandevere." Holt's tone was low, but urgent. "We know *why* he flew away. He recognized that other elephant's call."

"The one on Nightmare Island—that's his mother!" Milly piped up, unable to hide her excitement. Next to her, Joe bounced on his toes.

"Kali the Destroyer?" Vandevere shook his head. "Impossible." She had been purchased because she'd killed someone at a circus. . . . A dark thought crossed his mind. Could it have been *Medici's* circus? Vandevere cursed silently—if he'd known, tonight's debacle could have been prevented, and he'd be fondling a healthy check right now.

"It's true. It's her," Holt said. "She was sold from our circus two months ago."

"Every child knows its mother, and they say elephants never forget," Milly explained matter-of-factly.

Vandevere suppressed a grimace. The child's love for scientific tidbits was a nuisance at the moment. He needed to think. He needed some quiet.

"They can be together now!" As though unable to contain his happiness, Joe flung his arms wide, nearly knocking over a lamp.

Vandevere glared into the distance and spoke to the room at large, his voice flat. "Why are there children in my office?"

"Mr. Vandevere, please." Milly clasped her hands together. "All Dumbo wants is his mother. Just reunite them and he'll do whatever you want!"

"No, he'll do whatever *she* wants," Vandevere said. "First rule of animal training is to separate them from their parents so they learn to answer only to you."

Milly's expression crumpled. "But don't you want Dumbo happy?"

Vandevere stalked over to the window, peering down at the fairgrounds below, which were still active, even this late at night.

"I want my audience happy. I want my animals

to be mine. Think I'd have gone and bought her if I thought she was related to him? This doesn't help me at all."

"But V. A., please—" Colette stepped forward.

"Who *doesn't* want something from me? One person. You show me one." Vandevere glared around the room. Joe's shoulders hunched under his scrutiny, but Milly raised her chin. Colette snapped her mouth shut.

"*They're* Dumbo's family now," he continued, gesturing out the window. "Six nights a week, five bucks a head. Their love is all he'll ever need."

Next to Milly, Joe's eyes were welling with tears. She put a protective arm around him, tugging him close.

Vandevere picked up his coat from his chair and paused in front of them. "Thank you, child, for your help—your so-called scientific method. But the most important part of growing up is learning how to go it alone."

With that, he swept from the room.

Down below, Vandevere found Skellig waiting by his car. The huntsman nodded—letting Vandevere know that Dumbo was secure in his pen, with no chance of getting loose again. At least one person knew how to handle things, Vandevere thought.

Shrugging into his coat, Vandevere paused as Sotheby held the car door open for him. "Get rid of the mother. You know where to take her." His eyes darted down to Skellig's feet. "Treat yourself to new boots."

Skellig's mouth twitched into a smile and he nodded again. "Yes, boss."

"But sir, you can't just kill her," Sotheby objected.

"Why not? Who will ever know?" One problem solved, as far as Vandevere was concerned.

* * *

Milly's fingers rubbed the key on her necklace, her mind whirling from the past few minutes. She missed her mother more than ever. She'd know what to do. How could Vandevere think Mrs. Jumbo would cause trouble? Having her close would make Dumbo so happy—and he would still fly for them. She knew it in her heart.

If they took her away from him now, it would destroy Dumbo. Nothing could replace the love of his mother. Couldn't Vandevere see that?

Milly turned to Holt, her heart squeezing painfully. "Dad, do something. Please?"

Holt exchanged a look with Medici. Of course Vandevere had been too good to be true. In signing on to his amusement park, they'd given him power over all their lives. Vandevere didn't seem like the type to change his mind, but Holt had to at least try. For Milly and Joe. And for Dumbo. He plopped his cowboy hat on his head and jogged out the door.

He caught up to the Dreamland owner just as Vandevere was settling into his expensive car.

"Mr. Vandevere," Holt called out. "Please hear me out."

He stopped by the car and Vandevere turned cold eyes on him.

"Don't separate them, please. Don't do that to my kids." Holt tugged his hat off, practically begging.

Vandevere let him stew in silence for several seconds before answering. "You know, when my father left us it was a blessing, really, because I had to learn how to fend for myself. Maybe that's what your children need?" He raised an eyebrow at Holt, who bristled and clenched his fist.

"Don't tell me what my children need," Holt said.

"Best take a step back, elephant man," Skellig drawled, angling to be in front of Vandevere.

Behind Holt, Milly, Joe, Medici, and Colette rushed toward them. He felt their eyes on him.

"A circus is more than just a business," Holt said.

Even now, he believed with all his heart that it should be a community, a family, a home.

"Ah." Vandevere grinned at him, then shot a glance at Medici. "That must be why yours failed." Turning back to Holt, he arched his eyebrow in challenge. What would Holt do next?

Holt's lips pinched together. He wanted to draw the line in the dirt, demand Mrs. Jumbo move into the tent with Dumbo, but Vandevere could strip him of his job. Now that Colette knew Dumbo's training secrets, Holt was replaceable. He'd have no way to feed Milly and Joe. No place for them to stay. Who would hire a one-armed man?

Seeing the defeat in Holt's eyes, Vandevere smirked and addressed Milly.

"Darling, Dumbo and his mother need a little alone time. So Mommy is going on a little trip so that Dumbo doesn't get distracted."

Milly's face transformed from hope to horror as she realized what he meant. She glanced up at her dad, but he just looked back at her, remorse in his eyes. With a cry, she dropped her bag and took off into the crowd.

"Milly, wait!" Holt called, hurrying after her.

* * *

Colette ran over to Joe and hugged him close to keep him from chasing after his family and getting lost. Colette hoped Milly wouldn't go too far. She had looked so upset—and for good reason. Colette studied Vandevere, who was smiling smugly as he settled into the car. Skellig and Sotheby took their places as well, ever-constant bookends at his side.

What had gotten into V. A.? She'd never seen him as upset as he'd been upstairs, yelling and threatening. Nothing like his usual smooth-talking self. She knew the show always came first for him, but still, to tear a mother and child apart was heartless.

"Get in, Max," Vandevere ordered from the car. Head hung low, Medici trooped over and slid into his seat. Vandevere smirked, then held out his hand to his starlet. "Coming, Colette?"

She took a step back. "I have rehearsal."

Vandevere studied her for a moment, then nodded. "Yes, better get that act perfect," he said. Then he waved to Sotheby and the car rolled away.

*That felt good,* Colette thought as she turned back to Joe. He was crouched on the ground, gathering up the papers that had spilled from Milly's bag. She bent to help. Horses and a glittering couple galloped across every page—these were old promotional photos of Holt's act. They'd been ripped in half and then taped back together. Colette ran her fingers down the jagged line of one. The woman was lovely—her cheeks just as round as Joe's, her smile a mirror of Milly's.

Holt's act hadn't been a solo affair. His wife, Milly and Joe's mother, had ridden beside him. Understanding crashed over Colette.

"He's just a little elephant," Joe said, sniffling.

Colette pulled him into a hug. This was about more than one mother. "Oh, Joe, I'm so sorry." She wished there were something else she could do.

* * *

In the throngs of people, Holt searched for Milly, but she'd slipped away from him. He checked the Colosseum, the training tents, their new house, and the tents where the rest of the Medici troupe was staying. He trekked back to Nightmare Island, but it had been locked up for the night. Only the sounds of disgruntled beasts emerged from within, and Milly was nowhere to be seen.

Dejected, he circled back to the training tent. Dumbo was locked up in the golden carriage, snuffling pitifully. Joe was asleep on the ground next to it, his head in Colette's lap, but there was no sign of Milly. Holt sighed. He'd hoped that she'd come back here, to Dumbo.

"Did you find her?" Colette asked.

Holt shook his head. Where else could she be?

"It's not your fault," Colette said.

"I'm not sure it matters who's to blame. I just need to fix it is all."

"You will. You'll make her understand." Colette's face was full of confidence, but Holt wasn't so sure.

If only Annie were there. She knew how to talk to the kids, how to ease their heartache, make them understand what was happening. She would have found a way to convince Vandevere, too; Holt was sure of it.

"Her mama knew what to say, no matter what, she always knew. And I just can't seem to—the words don't come out right."

An awkward beat passed. Holt stared down at Joe. His son was curled into a ball and Holt could see tear tracks down his cheek. What could he tell them? How could he fix this?

"Your children don't need you to be perfect. They just need you to believe in them." Colette ran her hands through Joe's hair, smoothing it down.

"That simple, huh?"

Colette nodded at him.

Maybe she was right. Maybe there was a different kind of support his kids needed from him, not just food and shelter, but something deeper. Instead of wanting his kids to love what he loved, think like he thought, maybe he should listen and be there for them. Milly wasn't a performer; she loved science and solving puzzles through trial and error. Joe wasn't an artist who could pull off magic or acrobatic tricks, but he had a heart as wide and deep as the ocean, and this world could use more people like him. Holt might not be a rider anymore, might not be an elephant trainer if Vandevere decided to fire him, but no matter what, he would be the best father he could be.

Rather than preparing them for how harsh and cruel the world could be, he would be their shelter in the storm, a rock from which they could leap to find their own way.

Come to think of it, he had a pretty good idea where to find Milly, once the exhibit opened for the day. But for now, he'd keep searching.

Holt tipped his head to Colette and headed back out into the night.

* * *

Far across Dreamland, in a makeshift tent hotel, Milly sobbed as Catherine stroked her hair. She didn't want to see her father, not tonight. Not after he'd given up so easily. Not after he'd forfeited Dumbo's mother.

## CHAPTER SEVENTEEN

Once she'd fallen asleep, Catherine sent Ivan out to try to find Holt and let him know Milly had shown up after all and was safe now. Then she puttered around Milly, fetching blankets, remembering another night long ago when she'd felt helpless.

# IVAN THE WONDERFUL AND CATHERINE THE GREATER

## NORTH CAROLINA, JANUARY 1919

ain lashed the ground and battered the tents. Most of the troupe had retreated to the train, crowding into the boxcars to escape the worst of the storm, but Ivan and Catherine were braving the elements, despite the virulent strain of influenza ravaging their circus family.

"My love," Catherine said, curled into Ivan's side, "do you miss Florida?"

"They had hurricanes and plenty of storms there, too, mi amor," Ivan said.

"Yes." Catherine paused. "I was thinking more about the cottage on the bay."

"Ah." Ivan rubbed his jaw—something he did when he was uncomfortable.

He probably didn't want to think about the cottage. When they'd lived there, Catherine had decorated one of the rooms as a nursery, but they'd tried for years with no success to have children, even after they sold the cottage and joined the circus to see the country.

"We couldn't afford it anymore, remember? And we wanted the adventure of traveling," he finally said.

Catherine nodded, her face lined with sadness. The Medici troupe was wonderful; they stuck by each other through thick and thin, better even than some real families—better than her own, which had cast her out when she fell in love with Ivan, a Spanish immigrant and boardwalk magician. They had disapproved of the match.

But from the first time she'd seen him perform, his voice calling out over the backdrop of crashing waves, he'd tucked her heart up his sleeve just like a card. She'd watched for hours, eventually spotting his sleight of hand. Ivan had winked at her and touched his finger to his lips, pleading for silence. She'd learned Spanish for him—loving the way the words rolled through her mouth—and magic, as well. She was the finest magician's assistant to be found and had worked hard to master distraction and timing to boost Ivan's act.

"Catherine, Ivan, come quick!" Joe's voice cried out. "Help!"

Oh, no, Catherine thought.

Jumping up, the couple wrapped blankets around themselves, grabbed their meager medical supplies, and ducked out into the torrential rain to reach little Joe, who was shivering next to the train.

"Back inside, Joe, quickly," Catherine said, hustling him along.

The boxcar was nearly empty—just Milly and Pramesh hovered over Annie as she lay, trembling and pale, on a collapsible cot.

Annie's fever had finally broken the day before, and she'd even gotten to her feet. But she must have taken a turn for the worse that morning. A wretched cough racked Annie's body, and Milly helped her sit up, pressing a handkerchief to her mother's mouth. The white cloth came away spotted with blood.

Catherine cursed silently and moved to Milly's side, laying a protective hand on her shoulder as she knelt next to her.

"What can we do?" Ivan asked. Joe's eyes were a mix of hope and fear as he looked up at him.

Catherine felt a pang. Did he think Ivan had the magic to fix his mother? She wished Holt were there to comfort his children, to be by Annie's side.

Pramesh turned to Catherine with somber eyes. "I was hoping you might have some paraldehyde left."

Catherine dug through their bag for the vial, her hands trembling slightly as she handed it over. It might help ease the cough, but from the look in Pramesh's eyes, he meant it more as a salve to Annie's pain than as a cure.

With careful movements, Milly folded the handkerchief and set it aside, readying a new cloth in its place. Her lips were pressed tightly together, as if holding in her sorrow, but even without tears, it spilled out of her eyes as she bent to help her mother sit up enough to take the medicine.

Pramesh measured out a few drops, which Annie swallowed before slumping back into Milly's lap. In the back of the car, Joe was unusually still.

"My loves, come where I can see you," Annie pleaded.

Catherine took over for Milly so she and Joe could kneel on either side of Annie.

"Milly, Joe, you are the best things I've done." Annie paused to wheeze. "There is much more waiting for you. I know that you will accomplish amazing things—things I cannot even dream of!"

"Mama, no, please don't say that." Milly's voice quavered.

"Shh, my sweets. Listen, Joe, my kind boy, no matter what you do, remember to lead with your heart—it knows the way. Milly, my clever girl, the world may tell you no someday, but just remember you can unlock any door."

Annie's fingers tapped the key she'd given Milly just after Holt had shipped off to war.

"I'm so proud of you both," Annie whispered.

*Sobbing, Milly and Joe leaned over, hugging their mother. She held them to her tightly.*

*Her eyes met Catherine's above her.*

*"Take care of them, please," Annie said. "Until Holt comes home."*

*Catherine read the rest of Annie's message in her face:* If he doesn't make it back, if the war claims him, please take care of my children.

*"We will keep them safe and love them like our own," Catherine assured her. She dripped some water into Annie's mouth and ran her hand over her forehead.*

*Milly and Joe were still crying, but their mother slowly slipped into sleep, the paraldehyde taking effect.*

*"Is she—" Milly sat up, her face blotchy.*

*"No, my dear, she's sleeping," Catherine said. "Get some rest, little one."*

*With a respectful nod to Catherine and Ivan, Pramesh silently left for his own boxcar. Next to Joe, Ivan's expression was grim, but he gently rubbed the boy's back until Joe fell asleep. Milly, too rattled, kept vigil until her mother's chest stilled, her lungs giving out one final exhale.*

*Milly's face crumpled, but before the tears dropped, Catherine was there, wrapping her in an embrace, tugging her close and rocking her back and forth, back and forth.*

*"Shhh, shhhh, mi hija," Catherine whispered. "I've got you, I've got you."*

*Meeting Ivan's eyes, Catherine stifled a cry. They had been called upon to be guardians for a little while, and they would do their best.*

*Catherine bowed her head, kissing Milly's thick brown hair.* Whatever it takes, I will be here for you, *she thought fiercely.* As much as you'll let me.

# CHAPTER
# EIGHTEEN

From his window, Medici scanned Dreamland. They hadn't opened for the day yet, but workers bustled below, sweeping the paths and hauling water and food for the animals. He twirled a ring on his finger—a nervous habit. Everything was so much bigger here. But was bigger always better? At what cost?

*Thump.* Medici whirled to see Verna dropping a stack of pink papers on his desk. Finally, something for him to do.

Medici picked up the top one. Big letters proclaimed: CONTRACT TERMINATED. The name on the form was Rongo's.

"Whoa, whoa, what's this?"

"Gimme a break," his secretary snapped. "I gotta teach you to read English, too?"

Medici tore through the rest of the pile, then grabbed up the stack, his pulse racing, and hurried into Vandevere's office.

"Morning, Max," Vandevere said calmly. He set down the newspaper he was reading and selected a slice of orange from the breakfast spread in front of him. Glancing up, he saw the slips in Medici's hand. "Good, you got the paperwork. I finished reviewing the rest of your acts, and to be honest, they're pale imitations of ones we already have." Medici's stomach clenched, but Vandevere carried on like he was reciting the weather. "So one month's severance seems more than fair. *Capisci?*"

The papers grew damp in Medici's palm. "I thought you promised—"

"Tut, tut." Vandevere picked up a spoon and stirred a lump of sugar into his coffee. "The contract says I'd hire them . . . it never specifies for how long."

Was the floor swaying under him? Medici nearly stumbled. "But they're my troupe. They were counting on me." Miss Atlantis, Pramesh, Rongo, Puck, the rest . . . they were his people. He owed them.

Vandevere shrugged. "What does history value,

Max? The pyramids? Or the hands who built them?" He nodded at the slips. "That said, let's have a heart: they should hear the news from you."

That's what Vandevere called having a heart? Medici tried to object one more time, pointing out how valuable they could be, even as understudies. But Vandevere set down his cup and stared hard at him.

"Don't make this more difficult than it needs to be, Max. We can't take on every circus performer in the business. It should be the crème de la crème only for Dreamland. Don't forget, we're here to make dreams come true, magic come alive, the impossible possible. You had a good run with your crew, but they are nowhere near the caliber of the performers I've recruited from across the country. You have to face facts."

Resigned, Medici nodded and slunk from the room. He had no idea how to break this to his troupe. He'd need an hour to come up with something—maybe have leads on where they could go next or, well, something. But his heart dropped as soon as he approached his office. It looked as though he didn't have that luxury.

Crowded inside were Pramesh, Miss Atlantis, Puck, Ivan, Catherine, and Rongo. Someone must have summoned them all there. Medici gritted his teeth.

Rongo had been leaning against the wall, but he

straightened as Medici trundled in. "'Bout time, boss. So, when do we start?"

Their faces were full of excitement, their hopes high. But their time at Dreamland would end with crushed expectations. And it was all his fault. Medici sighed. Time to break some hearts.

\* \* \*

Light dusted the eastern horizon as Holt made his way to the Wonders of Science exhibit. Dreamland wasn't open for the day yet, but the cleaning crews had been through, unlocking buildings. He searched rooms of inventions until he found her.

Milly was staring at a life-sized statue of Marie Curie, glass test tubes gripped in her hands, an audience of wax scientists arrayed behind her. A plaque next to the display proclaimed her achievements—winner of two Nobel Prizes, discoverer of polonium and radium, and, Holt read with a jolt, creator of mobile radiography to enable field hospitals to have X-ray capabilities. He'd seen that used in the war.

Milly's eyes were full of yearning, her fingers running absently over the key Annie had given her.

"That's my daughter, all right: runs away to go to school," Holt said.

"It's our fault. The whole experiment." Milly hung her head.

A stab went through Holt at her expression. He crouched down next to her and patted her knee. "Nah, those are like people. They fail all the time."

"I bet Dumbo wishes he never met us," she said.

"You showed him he could fly. Do you think he'd ever trade that?" Holt asked.

"He would to have his mom back," Milly said without hesitation.

Holt nodded. He squeezed onto the bench next to her, tucking Milly into his side with his right arm.

Milly snuggled in closer. "I miss Mama," she said.

Holt leaned his head down to touch hers. "So do I." He squeezed her tight, both of them thinking of Annie.

After a few minutes, Milly sat up and looked at him, a glint he couldn't read in her eyes. "There's something I want to show you," she said.

Taking his hand, she led the way through exhibits about magnetic forces and wind power to a diorama showing a gleaming white kitchen, where an animatronic person stood opening a can. But the hand holding the can was made of metal.

Milly pressed the button next to the scene and a tinny voice emerged from a speaker.

"All kinds of new technological marvels await us in the twentieth century. With advances in both engineering and medicine, the mortal and mechanical will soon be combined to assist ordinary families, workers, and veterans and make them even stronger than they ever were before."

Tears stung Holt's eyes as he saw the figure pivot and place the can on the table, its metallic fingers releasing it one by one. Maybe one day soon science would create prosthetic limbs for people like him. Maybe Milly would be the scientist to do it. He squeezed her shoulder.

"Thank you." Holt smiled at her. "Now, let's get back to Dumbo. He needs us."

# CHAPTER
# NINETEEN

s they approached Dumbo's tent, they saw a crowd of people ducking inside, Miss Atlantis and Rongo among them. It seemed to be some sort of gathering for Medici's troupe. Colette ducked out of the tent and spotted Holt and Milly. With a worried face, she waved them over.

The Farriers hurried in, Colette at their side. There, they found Joe watching everything nervously. He flung his arms around Holt when he saw him.

Across the tent, Pramesh stood near Dumbo's pen, Tanak draped around the man's neck as usual. Pramesh held open a colorful silk bag as the troupe formed a line in front of him. Each person stepped up and carefully took out a single feather.

"Colette, what's going on?" Holt asked.

"Vandevere's cancelled their contracts. They're to leave by tomorrow." Her arms wrapped around her stomach.

"What?" Milly cried.

They crossed over to where the troupe was one by one laying down a feather near Dumbo. But the little elephant was too despondent to notice or care. Even though he wasn't in the golden carriage anymore, he was slumped on the floor.

"This is outrageous. He can't do this!" Holt's gaze darted among his friends, his colleagues, his family—including Dumbo.

Pramesh shrugged and smiled sadly. "All this doesn't mean anything to us. But no regrets, for we met true magic." He looked to the elephant. "Goodbye, little friend."

"We wanted to see him one last time," Rongo explained.

Miss Atlantis took Puck's elbow. "One last time to see him fly." Her voice caught and Puck patted her hand.

"I don't think he wants to anymore," Milly said.

Dumbo's ears hadn't so much as twitched since they'd approached, and his trunk lay flopped on the hay. His eyes were fixed on the wall of the tent as though he hoped it would disappear.

"Oh, no, but he must," Ivan cried.

Catherine nodded. "He just can't lose Mrs. Jumbo again."

"I'm afraid it's rather worse than that," a voice said sadly.

They spun to find Sotheby, top hat in hand, walking toward them.

"Mr. Sotheby? What are you doing here?" Colette asked.

Milly had never seen him more than ten steps from Vandevere, but thankfully his boss was nowhere in sight.

"Clearing my conscience." Sotheby paused and collected a feather from Pramesh's bag, keeping his hands well clear of the snake coiled around Pramesh's neck. "I resigned my position as soon as I heard him give the order."

"What are you talking about?" Holt asked. "What order?"

"Mrs. Jumbo will be gone by tomorrow night. And she's not meant to survive."

Milly and Joe clasped hands at Sotheby's words, and Colette tensed. The whole of Medici's troupe gaped in horror. Who would do such a thing?

Hanging his head, Sotheby slowly laid down his feather next to the others, then tipped his hat and left.

Colette opened her mouth. "V. A. wouldn't—" Then she paused, her face shadowed in doubt. Shaking her head, she dropped her gaze, then gasped. "Look at him—he understands," she said, gesturing to Dumbo, who had tears pooling in his eyes.

Holt clambered into the pen and sank down next to the elephant, wiping away his tears. He stroked Dumbo's trunk, tears in his own eyes. "This 'Dreamland' doesn't deserve him."

"No circus does," Colette declared.

Murmurs of agreement ran through the troupe.

Holt stood and faced them, his eyes meeting theirs. "Then who's gonna be willing to help me set Dumbo and his mother free?"

Milly's and Joe's mouths dropped open. He was serious! And if anyone could help Dumbo, it was him. Their dad was a hero.

"Let's see what we can find out and meet back here tonight." Holt divided up tasks and everyone set out.

\* \* \*

That night, the group reconvened in the tent, huddled together. Dumbo rolled onto his feet and stuck his trunk over the fence to watch them.

"I got some information from our old friend Sotheby," Holt said. "A truck is coming to take her at eight o'clock."

"Eight? That's right before the show!" Miss Atlantis bit her lip.

"Well, we've got to intercept that truck and somehow sneak her out of here." Holt was resolute. He laid down a map of the city.

"We can't hide an elephant in New York City," Rongo said, his face incredulous.

"Two elephants," Puck interjected. "Don't forget Dumbo."

"A cousin of mine has a cargo ship that sails tomorrow night, bound for Bombay." Pramesh pulled out a folded paper and set it down atop the map. Milly and Joe peered closer—it was a schedule for all the ships coming and going from the port that night. Pramesh pointed to one line. "If you can get them to the port, I promise you I'll take them home."

"Pramesh, you'd really go with them?" As eager as Milly was to set Dumbo and Mrs. Jumbo free, this would mean a true disbanding of their troupe.

"I miss my land, my history," Pramesh said

wistfully. Then he shot a mischievous look at Holt. "But if you wish to keep my snakes . . ." He unwound the python from his neck and held it out to the cowboy.

"Nope." Holt shook his head. "No, thank you. Nope."

"But how do we get Mrs. Jumbo past the park gates? They're all electrically controlled from the tower, and there's no way we can get up there," Colette pointed out.

"No, but Dumbo can." Holt smiled at her, finally revealing the last part of his plan. "If we can free him from the Colosseum, you two can *fly* there."

"Umm . . ." Colette was stunned. "This depends on me?" She cast her eyes on the elephant, who, truthfully, didn't look like he'd be flying anytime soon. Dumbo was slumped in despair.

Milly climbed into the pen to give him a hug.

"Hang on, Holt," Rongo spoke up, his voice a deep rumble of concern. "She still works for Vandevere, doesn't she?"

Medici's troupe members shifted uncertainly, but Holt's eyes were fixed on Colette's.

"Dumbo trusts her. So do I." He gave her a nod. Colette blushed.

Milly stared at her—she'd never seen the aerialist

blush before. But she agreed with her dad; Colette was trustworthy.

Holt turned to the others. "Open those gates and it's a race to the seaport. Impossible? Make it possible. C'mon, how hard can it be?"

Holt's grin was contagious, and everyone laughed when Barrymore swung down and plopped Holt's hat onto his head. Now the cowboy looked just like his old self.

Every person in the tent—Milly, Joe, the Medici troupe, and Colette—nodded. A thrill ran through Milly. Tonight, they would make a real dream come true. Dumbo's dream.

# CHAPTER
# TWENTY

ravel crunched under the wheels of the armored truck as it slowed to a stop by the Dreamland gates. Leaning out his window, the driver stated his assignment—pickup from Nightmare Island. Up in the tower, a Dreamland guard double-checked the schedule, then buzzed him through, unlocking the gates with a switch on his console.

The truck moved through the gates and cut down the back roads to Nightmare Island as the guard closed the gates behind it.

Inside the menagerie building, Vandevere, Medici, and Skellig waited for the truck while handlers removed all the clothing from Mrs. Jumbo. There was no telling if they'd get another "Kali" in to exhibit at some point.

Medici's stomach churned and he wished he had the strength of Sotheby, who'd mysteriously quit. This business with Mrs. Jumbo being shipped away was distasteful. Yes, he'd done it himself in a fit of passion after Rufus's death, but since then he'd reexamined things, and perhaps he'd acted rashly. Perhaps Mrs. Jumbo wasn't dangerous after all. She certainly seemed harmless now. Maybe even sad, he observed, as she dipped her head so the handlers could take off her headpiece.

"See, the great men, Max, the legends," Vandevere said, "they all must abandon their families."

As though she understood his words—and heartily disagreed—Mrs. Jumbo raised her trunk and trumpeted at Vandevere. Her glare did not shake him.

"You have to separate yourself, Max. Stand alone. You do that and history will remember your name," Vandevere continued.

Behind his back, Medici shot him a dumbfounded look. People didn't become famous for abandoning their families. Infamous, maybe. He guessed that's what he'd be if word spread about what he'd done to his troupe. But more than that, he couldn't believe he'd allowed this tycoon to send them packing—good, hardworking people with talents to share with the world.

"Come, Max," Vandevere said. "We have a show to attend. Remington and his friends are waiting. Everything must go smoothly tonight. Or we won't get the loan we need to buy out any remaining competition and pay off the builders and vendors we still owe money to."

You *still owe money to*, Medici thought, but he kept his mouth shut and followed Vandevere to the Colosseum.

\* \* \*

Backstage, Milly and Joe flanked Dumbo. They'd had to wheel him over in his chariot, as he refused to walk, and it had taken six adults to heft him into the carriage. Now the elephant was sprawled on the floor, his ears covering his face to block out the sounds of the cheering crowd.

"Come on, Dumbo, get up," Milly coaxed. "You've gotta fly tonight!"

"It's your most important show," Joe said.

Holt came to stand by his kids, worry creasing his forehead. "What if he won't perform now for Vandevere? How do we make him understand?"

Milly knelt down next to Dumbo, peeling back his ears so he had to meet her eyes. She held up her necklace. "Locks turn, doors open. Tonight we're bringing your mom to you."

Hope flickered in Dumbo's eyes and he lifted his head. Holt and Joe nodded behind Milly, all three shining with expectation. Colette joined them, her face bright.

"Who's been dreaming like I've been dreaming?" Vandevere boomed. He sauntered into the backstage area and took Colette's hands in his.

She twisted her face away as he leaned in to kiss her cheeks. "V. A., please, my makeup," she said. She lifted one of her gloved hands, and he reluctantly kissed that instead.

Straightening, he turned to Holt. "Precision tonight, Farrier. Clockwork."

"That's what it's gonna take," Holt agreed, thinking of all the moving pieces in their scheme. Hopefully the rest of the troupe was doing all right on Nightmare Island.

"Any predictions from our scientist?" Vandevere asked Milly.

"Never let anyone tell you what you can't do," she said, parroting his words back to him.

Vandevere nodded his agreement, "Yes, indeed.

Nothing can stand in our way." Then he crouched next to Dumbo, who was at least sitting up now. He gazed into Dumbo's black eyes and smiled.

"Fly, Dumbo! Fly like you've never flown before." Apparently satisfied with his inspirational pep talk, Vandevere said goodbye to the others and strode off to find his distinguished guests.

* * *

Across the park, Medici's troupe crouched in shadows, watching as the armored truck crossed the bridge over the moat surrounding Nightmare Island and backed into the building. Now they just had to wait until Mrs. Jumbo was loaded.

"Are you ready?" Rongo asked Miss Atlantis.

"I'm no Puck here," Miss Atlantis said, nudging the actor, whose face turned red, "but melodramatic I can do."

Puck cleared his throat. "Um, break a leg—I mean, tail."

Miss Atlantis smiled at him. "Don't worry. I can keep that guard occupied until you get out with Mrs. Jumbo."

On the bridge to Nightmare Island, two patrolmen straightened and peered out as a figure emerged from the night. Miss Atlantis staggered onto the planks, clutching a fake mermaid tail to her chest.

"Sorry, ma'am, attraction's closed," a guard told her.

Ignoring him, Miss Atlantis swooped past, her expression one of despair.

"My dream was to be a mermaid, and now they've taken it away," she cried dramatically. "And yet . . . I hear the waters singing. I hear them beckoning me home."

The guard hurried after her as she stepped to the edge of the bridge, arms flung wide.

"Ma'am, please get ahold of yourself."

"Return me to the vast abyss," Miss Atlantis proclaimed, her voice reverberating in the wind. "My destiny—the sea!"

The guard reached for her just as she flung herself forward, and he toppled down with her—both landing with a splash in the moat below.

"Mmmf, lady," the guard sputtered as she flopped on top of him, "it's only four inches deep."

As they flailed, the second guard approached and peered over the edge. Miss Atlantis's hand reached up and pulled him in as well.

Coast clear, Medici's troupe snuck over the bridge,

their costumes and equipment held tight. Rongo used his strength to pull back the bars of the gate. Puck whistled low, impressed at the strongman, then gestured the others forward. Once the gap was wide enough, Harold, also known as the Rubberband Man, bent his thin body through. From the other side, he pulled a lever, opening the gate. The troupe scurried through, careful to close the gate behind them.

* * *

The stage manager called for Dumbo to take his position. Holt saddled Dumbo up and looked into his eyes.

"All right, Big D. All up to you." He addressed his kids next. "Soon as he gets airborne, run back to his tent and I'll find you there." Holt had a feeling it would be chaos once Dumbo got out, and he wanted Milly and Joe clear of the Colosseum in case the crowd stampeded. They nodded up at him, their faces earnest. He kissed their heads, hoping he'd be able to make them proud tonight.

He stepped over to grab his jacket and hat, oblivious that the motion dislodged his fake arm, which slid off.

"Holt," Colette said. She gestured to the arm on the ground.

Holt picked it up, weighing it in his hand. "Ah, to heck with it." He tossed it aside. He was done with useless appendages.

Colette smiled in delight. Stepping over to him, she helped him pin up his sleeve.

"We could have used a little rehearsal," she whispered so the kids wouldn't hear.

"A rehearsal? Think at the Battle of the Argonne we got a rehearsal?" Holt joked. But then he studied her. "Sure you can do this?"

"Oh, I fly elephants all the time," Colette said breezily, before arching an eyebrow at him. "Are you sure *you* can do this?"

Holt grinned. "With one hand tied behind my back."

Colette rolled her eyes and nudged him away. They had an elephant to steal.

* * *

Inside the Nightmare Island zoo, Ivan slipped one of his wands through the bars around the electrical panel. With a nudge, he turned up the fog machine, which let out a hiss of air. The mist thickened. Swinging his wand to hook a lever, he tugged.

*Bam!* They were all plunged into darkness.

"What the heck? We just lost power," one of the island guards said.

"To everything?" The armored truck driver sounded nervous. "Even the cages?"

*Bang! Bam! Wham!* From the sounds of it, the animals were ramming against their doors to get out. Maybe they could smell the guards' fear.

A grizzly bear's growl rumbled. The lion's roar called back.

"Where are the breakers? Get these lights back on!" Skellig ordered. Shaking his head at the quivering of the men beside him, he slammed the rear doors of the truck closed on Mrs. Jumbo and headed off to find the panel himself.

Wanting to get away, the truck driver stepped up to the cab of the truck, but something within moved. The seat was covered in snakes.

With a piercing shriek, the driver retreated. Arav chuckled as Catherine and a few others slipped into the back of the truck. He'd collect the snakes before joining them.

The place was full of fog—floor to ceiling. The guards saw the silhouettes of predators stalking free: a lion, a bear, and a crocodile.

Skellig couldn't believe the animals could have escaped that easily. How had they not attacked already?

Pushing the men in one direction, Skellig stalked off in the other. One of them would find the switches.

One of the guards reached the breakers.

*Pop!* The lights came back up. Skellig blinked, then blinked again. The creatures prowling around them were Medici's acrobats in animal costumes, and another of the troupe growled into a megaphone.

"It's a trick! Get back to the—" Skellig bellowed, but it was too late.

*Vrooom.* The truck's engine revved and it plowed forward, Ivan swinging up onto the back as it burst through the doors of the building.

Skellig and the guards raced after it. "Stop that truck!" Skellig yelled. But the moat's guards were not at their post. They were helping a dripping Miss Atlantis back onto the bridge.

Spotting the truck, Miss Atlantis kicked one of the guards into the moat and thwacked the second one with her tail, knocking him back into the water. "Sorry," she called.

Rongo slowed the truck just long enough for Miss Atlantis to swing aboard and join him and Puck in the cab.

"Those animal impressions were terrific, Puck," Rongo said.

Puck chuckled. "Well, the acrobats really mimicked their movements so well—if I hadn't known it was them, I would have thought the critters got out, too!"

"Who says a circus needs real animals?" Rongo said.

"Yeah, who says you need 'em at all?" Puck answered.

They all traded looks, an idea brewing. Something that could be spectacular.

# V. A. VANDEVERE

## NEW YORK CITY, 1919

*ool wind off the ocean cut through the oppressive summer heat, although V. A. refused to allow such a trifling thing as the weather to affect him as he strolled through his pride and joy, Dreamland. Glancing down, he tucked his favorite gold pocket watch into the vest of his three-piece suit.*

*A watch he had bought himself, with his own earnings, not anything he'd inherited from his father. His lip lifted in an involuntary snarl at the thought of the man.*

*All through his childhood, V. A.'s father had berated and belittled him. He mocked his grades at school, his lack of friends, and his piano performances—a musical endeavor his mother insisted upon despite her complete lack of interest in anything else having to do with her son. Of course, the old man had gotten his in the end—fired from his job at the law firm for annoying the wrong high-profile client.*

*Unemployed, his father had spiraled downward as their bank account ran dry, lashing out at his wife and son until he'd finally snapped, stalked out of their house, and moved to Montana, looking for gold. He'd never found any, of course. And now V. A. took a secret twisted pleasure in reading his father's letters pleading for money. He'd wire a small amount to his father every fourth request or so, dangling just enough to keep his father hoping for more.*

*He'd been more generous with his mother while she was alive. A socialite from old money who knew how to charm and little else, V. A.'s mother drifted after his father left. Only sixteen, V. A. had stepped up, spinning small jobs like hawking theater shows into bigger ones— writing the flyers for those very same shows, working backstage, and finally making his way up to director. Of course, his mother's family had disapproved, but there wasn't much they could do.*

*Over the years, V. A. learned the ins and outs of showmanship. He had a keen eye for what motivated people and could spot talent from a hundred yards away. Nobody could match his marketing savvy, either. It had taken him a decade, but he'd been able to sock away enough to launch Dreamland—a place where magic happened and childhood dreams came true.*

*And now, his own dreams were in danger. The contractor for the roller coaster was insisting on full payment rather than split deposits, the loan he'd used to buy out the Zuckerman circus was multiplying in interest faster than his ticket sales, and postproduction costs on his last film were triple what he'd been quoted.*

*He needed an infusion of excitement into Dreamland—something big and bold and never seen before.*

*Leaning back against the fence behind him, V. A. surveyed his grand park. What was missing?*

*"V. A., there you are," Sotheby's voice called.*

*"What's the news, Sotheby?" V. A. asked. It couldn't be good if his trusted assistant was tracking him down.*

*Sotheby's expression was rueful as he approached. Yes, definitely bad news.*

*"The electric company sent over a representative. If next month's bill isn't paid up front, he says they're going to cut the power."*

*Dreamland couldn't run without electricity. Everything from the gates to the rides to the lights in the tents needed it. It had taken seven electricians to install the special set of transformers that processed all the power Dreamland used on a nightly basis.*

*"A representative, huh?" V. A. mused. He liked dealing with people face to face. It was much easier to read them in person than via letter or over the phone. Maybe this representative had a wish V. A. could fulfill. Perhaps he had children who'd love a free VIP night at the circus,*

*complete with behind-the-scenes introductions to the acrobats. Or perhaps the representative was an aspiring actor—V. A. could find a role for him in his next film. V. A. had connections everywhere. He'd make something happen.*

*All he had to do was find out what the man dreamed of and make it come true.*

*"I'll come talk to him," V. A. told Sotheby. "Please escort him to the Manhattan dining room and let him know I'll be there presently."*

*"Very good, sir. Shall I have Diane prepare a meal? Or just some beverages?"*

*"Let's do light refreshments. Those crab cakes she made last week were exquisite." V. A. paused, watching the waves. "Oh, and Sotheby, see if Colette is available to join us."*

*She was almost as good as he at charming people, and her graceful poise always relaxed V. A., let him shine at his best.*

*Sotheby bowed his head in salute and headed back to the Dreamland headquarters.*

*He could fix all this. He'd clawed his way out of deeper holes before. V. A. inhaled deeply, letting the ocean scent clear his head.*

*First step, charm the power company representative into a new payment plan. Next up, secure a second loan;*

*perhaps mortgage his mother's house on the cape. There was a banker he'd met last month at the museum gala . . . Remington. That was it. Maybe he'd be interested in investing in the grand amusement park.*

*As he worked on all that, V. A. would keep an eye out for the next biggest star act. There'd been rumors of a giant hairy man living in the mountains out West. Rumblings from Russia spoke of performers looking to relocate en masse in light of tighter government control. He'd also seen an article the other day on a woman in Delaware who supposedly commanded the weather. He somehow doubted that last one, but V. A. was thorough in his quest for greatness. No stone would be left unturned.*

*Who knew? Maybe tomorrow's paper would hold the key to his dreams.*

*No matter how long it took or where his search took him, he would find a gem to raise Dreamland above all other circuses, menageries, and fairgrounds. Once he did, he'd never let it go.*

## CHAPTER
# TWENTY-ONE

From the back of the VIP booth, Medici watched the show, the lights following the performers perfectly, the audience in the tent gasping at all the right places. And they hadn't even seen Dumbo yet.

"Mr. Medici? May I show you to your seat?" the coat check girl asked politely. She eyed the suitcase in his hands, but Medici clutched it tighter, so she gestured toward the empty chair in the front row of the booth instead. Right next to Vandevere.

"No, why don't you take it?" Medici didn't want it, that was for sure.

"Oh, no, really, sir, I couldn't."

"Please, it's the best seat in the house."

"Oh, yes, sir, no question. But it's your circus," she said.

"Go on, you'll enjoy it," Medici urged.

Blushing, she thanked him and scampered down the aisle.

Looking over his shoulder, Vandevere noticed Medici and waved him forward. Yet Medici couldn't make his feet move.

Skellig burst into the booth at that moment. He'd been heading for Vandevere, but when he saw Medici, he grabbed hold of him instead.

"You!" Skellig whispered loudly.

Sensing an emergency, Vandevere smoothly nodded at his guests and slipped up the aisle to join them as Skellig hauled Medici into the stairwell.

"Where is your circus? Your circus of thieves?" Skellig shook Medici slightly, but Medici had no idea what he was talking about. His troupe had all been sent packing.

"What's going on here?" Vandevere asked.

"It's the elephant's mother. She's gone—and his troupe is behind it," Skellig explained, chest heaving in anger.

"What? They'd never!" Medici exclaimed. "They couldn't. Well, maybe . . ."

Medici cowered behind his briefcase as Vandevere and Skellig glared at him.

"Alert the tower, secure the gates," Vandevere ordered. "Don't let them get out." Then he paused. "But why would they only take the one?"

His face paled and he spun to the show, where Dumbo's act was about to start. "We have to keep an eye on Farrier—and his children," he ordered as a spotlight turned on, shining full blast on Dumbo, high above the crowd.

"You come with us, Medici. Fix it," Skellig said, grasping Medici's elbow and hauling him with them.

The trio stormed backstage, but Milly and Joe saw them coming and ducked behind a crate. As Vandevere and Skellig moved on, Medici noticed an open door to the outside. Curious, he ventured out.

There was Holt, bowie knife clasped in his mouth, scaling a ladder one-handed.

"You know, whenever you put that hat on it usually means trouble," Medici drawled.

Startled, Holt nearly lost his grip. His shoulders relaxed slightly—only slightly—when he saw it was Medici. Their gazes locked.

"Dumbo doesn't belong here. None of us do," Holt told him.

"Hey, you, what're you doing up there?" a guard called.

"Get down here," his partner yelled.

Medici regarded them coolly. "He is a maintenance man fixing the light. Get back to your posts," he ordered.

The men saluted as they left.

"Still know how to put on a show, don't you, Gustavo?" Holt smiled down at Medici.

"Still got hope." Medici grinned back at him. "Learned that from you."

Nodding, Holt began working his way higher up the building, clinging to the metal supports. For the first time since getting to Dreamland, Medici felt truly proud, the knot in his stomach finally untying.

\* \* \*

Inside the main tent, Colette spun higher in the air as the chandelier brought her to Dumbo's platform.

The elephant eyed her warily as she stepped onto it lightly. Colette smiled at him.

"Let's try this again. You and me," she said.

She climbed onto his saddle and held a single feather aloft for all to see before handing it forward to Dumbo. He reluctantly wrapped his trunk around it.

Then Colette projected her voice so the audience could hear her.

"Dumbo, Prince of the Elephants! I command you to fly with me!" she shouted.

Colette flung her arms out with a flourish, but Dumbo's ears stayed downcast. Desperate for him to understand, she leaned forward and whispered.

"Dumbo, please fly. Do it for your mama."

A shiver of excitement passed through Dumbo at the word *mama*, and he slurped the feather up his trunk. His chest puffed out as he sat up. Then he took two steps forward and plunged off the platform so quickly that Colette grabbed hold of the saddle with a small shriek of surprise.

The crowd gasped as the elephant and rider dropped, plummeting to the ground. Backstage, Milly and Joe hugged one another close, eyes riveted on the arena. Vandevere paused in his search for the Farriers to watch as well. Then . . .

*Fwoop.* Dumbo's ears flared wide and he swung up.

Colette cried out in delight as Dumbo soared around the tent. All the faces below her were turned up in awe, silently absorbing the miracle.

"It's happening," Vandevere whispered from the wings. His gaze moved from Dumbo and Colette to the crowd. "This is the dream."

From Dumbo's back, Colette spotted a slash in the tent fabric—Holt was on the other side, furiously sawing at the tough material to make the slit wider.

"There, Dumbo," Colette whispered, pointing. "Look for the stars."

Dumbo's head swiveled, his eyes lighting up at the beautiful glimmer of starlight beyond the hot lights of the tent. He angled toward it.

"Aaah!" A scream came from below. It sounded like Joe.

Colette arched her neck to see. Just out of sight of the spotlights, Vandevere and his thug, Skellig, had Joe and Milly cornered. The brutes were gripping the kids tightly.

"Dumbo, the kids," Colette urged.

Dumbo's ears had caught the scream as well and he pivoted, eyes picking out the trapped Milly and Joe. Huffing, he dove toward the men looming over them, Colette clinging to his back in terror.

At the last moment, Vandevere and Skellig sensed him coming and ducked out of the way, letting go of Milly and Joe. The kids seized their chance and bolted.

Vandevere growled as Dumbo and Colette flapped back up toward the ceiling. He turned to Skellig, snarling, "Get me those kids."

Skellig darted off while Vandevere fumed. High

above them, Dumbo wrapped his ears protectively around Colette and shot through the opening cut into the Colosseum, accidentally knocking Holt off-balance.

The cowboy bounced and rolled down the side of the tent, the ground getting closer every moment. Just before he reached the ledge, he grabbed hold of a railing, clinging to it like a life preserver.

Free in the open air, Dumbo's ears flared wide. The wind was stronger up there, but he adjusted quickly, banking to keep Colette sheltered.

She looked back, checking on Holt. He'd scaled the railing and was watching them. Facing forward, Colette scanned for their goal.

"Dumbo, there!" Colette pointed to the tower.

As they soared toward it, Colette flung off her wig and headdress—she wouldn't need them anymore. Tonight she would not only help free Dumbo and his mother, she would free herself as well.

# CHAPTER
# TWENTY-TWO

It was a routine night up in the tower for the two engineers: monitor the gate traffic and pull the switch to open it for vehicles when the guard below radioed; make sure none of the breakers popped from electrical overload; and basically sit back, relax, and take in the sparkling lights of Dreamland shining on a . . . flying elephant coming straight for them?

"What on earth?" one of the guards cried.

They both bolted to their feet as the elephant careened toward them. He wasn't slowing down.

"Aaaah!" The men dropped to the floor, covering their heads. But as Dumbo thunked into the window, it held strong, and he landed on the catwalk.

Colette leapt off the elephant and darted into the tower booth.

"Don't mind us, just passing through," she said sweetly, stepping over one of the guards to get to the controls.

"Hey! You can't do that." The bigger guard leapt to his feet and picked her up just as Colette reached for the MAIN PARK GATES switch.

Colette squirmed and kicked, but she couldn't break the man's hold. Turning her head, she fixed her eyes on Dumbo, who had poked his head into the booth.

"Dumbo, she needs you," Colette implored.

"*Eeeeuuggh!*" Dumbo trumpeted. He squeezed himself inside, nearly trampling the second guard.

Confidently, Dumbo wrapped his trunk around the switch and yanked it up.

*Clang!*

Down below, the golden gates of the park swung open, to the surprise of the crowd. People dove out of the way as a large truck, driven by a smiling bald man, burst out from behind a tent and tore past them and out the gates, gravel churning up from its wheels. The gate guards blinked in astonishment, then stared up at the tower.

Dumbo's eyes were alight with excitement; he toggled other switches and pulled every lever within reach.

"Get the elephant," the larger guard ordered.

"*You* get the elephant!" the smaller one countered.

After a quick estimation regarding the tonnage of said elephant, both men decided the best course of action was to let him be.

Across the park, sections of light flared out as Dumbo joyfully poked and prodded the controls. Colette could hear shrieks of fear and saw people stampeding out of the dark.

"Dumbo, I think that's enough," she said, nudging the elephant. Nuzzling her with affection, Dumbo cheerfully ignored her.

* * *

The lights in front of Milly and Joe flickered and popped off, throwing their path into darkness. The kids glanced up at the tower, where the silhouette of two large ears could be seen.

"They're there; they made it!" Joe cried happily.

The kids dashed down a shortcut to the training tent, but their dad wasn't there as they had planned earlier. The mice inside the miniature circus squeaked in alarm, so Joe hurried over to take them out, carefully tucking them in his pockets.

"Don't worry, Dad'll be here soon," Milly said, seeing the concern on Joe's face.

"I am counting on it." Skellig loomed in the doorway, a nightstick in his hand.

"Come on!" Milly yelled, tugging Joe behind her. The kids darted through a back entrance and into the mayhem of Dreamland.

They'd have to find their dad before Skellig did.

* * *

Pandemonium, crushed crowds, terrified audiences, lights flickering out all over his visionary park. A pit of anger stewed in Vandevere's heart. This was the cowboy's fault, he just knew it.

He seized two guards who were staring dumbfounded at the chaos.

"Get to the tower!" he screamed, giving them a little shove. "Why are you just standing there?"

"Electricity's out. No elevators," one replied.

Vandevere's eyes narrowed into slits and his voice got dangerously low. "The last time I checked, they had invented *stairs*."

Stalking past, he moved toward the tower himself, the two abashed guards quickly following.

Two hundred steps later, they reached the top catwalk. Vandevere barely paused to catch his breath, charging into the booth.

"What happened to my power?" he demanded.

Colette gave him a cheeky wave from behind Dumbo's back.

"What power, *mon cher*?" she said.

"Why, you ungrateful–" Vandevere spat. He couldn't reach her over the elephant's bulk, but he shook his fist, his cheeks bright red in rage. "You were nothing before I made you my, er . . ."

Colette glared coolly at him. "I believe the word is *queen*."

Pulling a feather from her costume, she held it out to Dumbo, whose eyes grew wide at the sight.

"Time to catch up with Mama. Hang on to that feather and fly!"

Dumbo wrapped his trunk around the feather and Colette swung onto his back. Vandevere and the guards had to duck as the elephant leapt out of the booth, soaring into the night sky.

Growling, Vandevere raced to the controls. The lousy engineers finally snapped out of their paralysis, shamefaced.

"Mr. Vandevere, wait!" One of the engineers started forward in alarm. "We have to reset the mains, or you could cause a surge."

"We need lights!" Vandevere insisted.

"Right now it's impossible," the engineer said.

"Nothing's impossible," Vandevere proclaimed.

Whatever Vandevere had dreamed up, he'd been able to make happen, and he wasn't going to let an ungrateful, spiteful performer and a motley troupe get in the way of his Dreamland.

Teeth bared in determination, Vandevere slammed up the switches.

"No!" the engineers called, but it was too late.

*Kerboom! Zzzzt!* Beneath the tower, the transformers boomed, sending a shower of sparks in all directions. Fiery embers skittered across the wooden planks of the platforms and rained down on the fabric tents nearby.

Vandevere watched in horror as several fires sprouted to life. No, this wasn't happening. Desperate, he stabbed at the controls.

*Zzzt!* The control panel itself sparked.

One of the guards rushed to the radio box and picked up the speaker, calling down to those below: "Get everyone out. Evacuate the park. And get the animals to safety."

"No, we can stop this. We'll save it." Vandevere slammed more buttons. "You can't destroy a dream!"

As the panel continued to spark, the guards hauled Vandevere away and down the stairs. From the stairwell, they could see the fire spreading.

Screams filled the air, then the shrill neighs of horses let loose as well.

* * *

People flooded through the gates. Frantically, Holt scanned their faces from the back of a horse—he'd freed all of them when he found the training tent smoking. Fires hadn't been part of the plan. He hoped nobody got hurt.

"Milly, Joe! I'm here," he shouted. Maybe they'd hear him or see him, since he was up above the crowd a bit.

Then he spotted them. Instead of running with the pack, they were plunging toward the Colosseum. And Skellig, that brute, was chasing after them.

"No, this way! Run to me!" Holt yelled, but he knew it was no use. They were too far to hear.

As he urged his steed against the press of people swarming the gate, a building next to the Colosseum caught fire. Flames licked the massive tent—it would be next. Clearly oblivious to this, his kids and Skellig raced into the structure.

The crowd started to part. Holt kicked his horse into a gallop and burst into the Colosseum just as Skellig cornered his kids.

"It's time you learned to follow orders," Vandevere's henchman growled. He snatched Milly in a rib-crushing grip.

A flush of rage ran through Holt and he unhitched his lasso, swinging it through the air. It caught on Skellig's free arm, which was reaching for Joe.

"Get your hands off my family," Holt growled.

With a sharp tug, Holt tightened the lasso and jerked Skellig to the ground, freeing Milly. Skellig yelped as he was dragged behind the horse. Holt looped his end of the rope around the saddle and tied it tight before swinging down and giving the horse a pat on the rump. Eager to escape the smoke seeping into the tent, the horse bolted out the door, taking a cursing Skellig with it.

Milly and Joe ran to their father, who tucked them in to his side. "Let's get out, the whole place is gonna—"

*Whoosh!* At that moment, a few of the stands burst into flame. The dry benches were the perfect kindling, and the fire quickly spread around the circle, trapping them. Even the exit curtains were burning.

The temperature seemed to jump a hundred degrees, and smoke started to fill the grand space. Sweating, Holt grabbed a nearby banner and tried to beat back the closest flames. The mice dug their claws into Joe's skin through his clothes and squeaked in fear. Milly searched for a way out, but the backstage area was consumed as well. A piece of blazing fabric crashed to the floor near them. Joe and Milly screamed, but Holt ran over, stomping on it to put it out. He hurried back to their side, clutching them tightly as they felt the temperature rise.

\* \* \*

A quarter mile away, Colette and Dumbo landed gracefully next to the waiting truck. Colette slid off as Dumbo, trumpeting wildly, galumphed into the truck to greet his mother. The two elephants chirped happily, trunks winding over and around each other, pressing into one another's sides. Finally, they were able to touch.

The Medici troupe burst into applause.

"We did it!" they cheered.

"Come on, to the seaport!" Rongo said, waving the performers onto the truck.

"Wait, where are the Farriers?" Colette asked.

Dumbo's ears perked up as a familiar scream pierced through the wail of sirens and pounding footfalls of the scattering crowd. *"Aaaaaaah!!!"*

That was Milly. His mother seemed to recognize the girl's voice as well.

Mrs. Jumbo ducked her head to look at her son,

then trumpeted a command. Dumbo blinked solemnly in agreement. After a final tap of his trunk to her forehead, as if to reassure himself she'd be there when he got back, Dumbo backed away. Whirling around, he clattered up to Colette and sucked a feather off her costume. The performers dove to the sides of the road as Dumbo galloped along.

Then the little elephant leapt into the air. Zooming over the gates, he dipped down to Nightmare Island and sucked up water, just as he'd done in the fire routine back at Medici's circus. He shot back into the air and flapped toward the sound of Milly's voice.

Soon he would be with his mama again.

But first, his help was needed.

# CHAPTER
# TWENTY-THREE

eat pressed in on the Farriers from all sides. Any minute now the central posts would crack and bring the whole burning tent down on them. They had to get out of there.

Holt wrapped the banner around his kids, positioning them in front of his body.

"Huddle tight. Cover up your faces. We're gonna make a run right out that door."

Trembling, Milly and Joe did as he said, drawing the banner over their heads.

"No one's coming. We're all we've got." Holt gripped his family with his one arm, praying that this would work. At least it was better than staying there, in the center of an inferno. "Cavalry charge on one, two—"

*Splooooosh!* A spray of water doused the entrance curtains long enough for an elephant to come crashing inside.

"Dumbo!" Milly squealed.

He tripped as he tried to land and tumbled, rolling to a stop at their feet, his face upside down. Beaming, the elephant staggered to a standing position and shook his ears out, splattering them with water.

Holt grinned. "Howdy, partner. I do love a clown act." The curtain wasn't quite as blazing now, thanks to Dumbo. Holt gathered his kids and hustled them forward. "Now's our chance. Run!"

The Farriers charged for the exit, Dumbo right beside them. As they approached the flaming fabric, Dumbo blasted it with the last reserves of the water he'd suctioned up.

*Puff.* His feather drifted out on the spray and was quickly caught in an updraft.

Still galloping next to the Farriers as they broke out into fresh air, Dumbo shot a look over his shoulder. Embers from the fire lit the feather and burned it to a crisp within seconds.

Holt gathered his kids in the safe open space between tents, kissing the tops of their heads. Then he scanned the area—people were still streaming out of the gates and most of the guards were guiding them out, their backs turned to the Farriers . . . for now. But Vandevere, stalking toward the men, spotted them.

"Get them," Vandevere yelled.

"They've seen us. Dumbo, you gotta go," Holt urged.

But Dumbo just stood there, ears drooping slightly.

"The feather." Realization hit Milly. "He lost the feather."

"The feather's what makes him fly," Joe explained as Holt looked lost.

Holt shook his head. "What? That feather doesn't do anything. Dumbo, you don't need the feather to fly. It's all you!"

Dumbo shrank away as Holt tried to nudge the elephant into the sky. His trunk flopped back and forth as he shook his head.

"Oh, no, they're coming," Joe said, pointing to several guards who were headed their way.

Holt absently tried to wring his hands together, then wiped his lone hand on his pant leg. "How's he ever gonna understand?"

Milly unhooked her necklace and crouched down in front of Dumbo, commanding his gaze. "Remember this?" she asked, holding up the key her mom had given her.

It was the most precious thing she owned. It was

what she'd believed connected her to her mother, what made her special.

She reached back and flung it into the Colosseum.

"Milly, no!" Joe cried.

"I can unlock any door. I can do it. *Me*," she said firmly. "You can, too."

Dumbo perked up, his eyes questioning Milly and darting between her earnest face and the burning tent where she'd tossed her talisman. He straightened his shoulders and let out a short trumpet blast.

The guards were shouting at one another now as they raced toward them. Vandevere's face was contorted in rage.

"Time to go, come on," Holt said, lifting Joe onto Dumbo's back. Then he scooped Milly up and dropped her next to her brother.

"Dad!" Milly said.

"What are you doing?" Joe asked.

Holt rubbed their heads one at a time. "Too much weight for all three of us. Get him to the seaport. You have to show him which way to go. I'll meet you there."

"That's my elephant! Stop them!" Vandevere bellowed.

Kneeling in front of Dumbo, Holt gazed into the elephant's eyes. He was entrusting his kids to this creature, but he had the utmost faith in him. "C'mon,

Big D. I believe in you, too," he said softly, tapping foreheads with Dumbo.

Holt stood and backed away as Dumbo flared his ears out and started thundering down the fairway, right toward the guards. Milly and Joe clung to the saddle as Dumbo pushed off the ground and swooped into the air.

"Yeeehaaaw!!" Joe cried. "We're flying! We're really flying!"

Wind whipped their faces as Dumbo cleared the Dreamland gates and circled through the air.

From Joe's pockets, three little mice poked their heads out and squeaked. But they seemed excited, not scared.

Milly and Joe looked at each other, soaking in the feeling of being so high up. Their noses and cheeks were pricked with cold, but down below, the city streets and apartments of New York unfurled like a miniature playset. And trundling along the road was an armored truck carrying Mrs. Jumbo.

"Follow that truck!" Milly called.

*"Eeeeugh!"* Dumbo trumpeted happily. His tail spun and he dove forward, ears flapping, heart thumping wildly in delight.

\* \* \*

On the ground, Holt breathed a sigh of relief—his kids and Dumbo were in the clear. Seeing an unattended police horse, Holt swung up on its back.

"You freak!" Vandevere spat, advancing on Holt with rage-filled eyes. "What have you done?"

"What they pay me for, mister." Holt tipped his hat. "Put on a hell of a show."

With a whistle, Holt steered his horse for the gate and galloped past Vandevere. The circus owner could do nothing but curse.

Dreamland crackled, fire leaping from tent to tent like an acrobat on the flying trapeze. Vandevere stared in disbelief. How had it come to this? The fire engines had arrived, along with mounted policemen, but even Vandevere, who believed in the impossible, didn't think they'd be able to salvage anything of his park.

As reporters and policemen approached him, Vandevere spotted Medici. He stormed over to him, jabbing his finger into the shorter man's chest.

"He stole my elephant! Arrest this man. This man right here." Vandevere's face was red. "We have a contract, Max Medici. I own you." Vandevere's voice lowered to an ominous rumble.

"Yeah." Medici shrugged, totally unconcerned. "You own Max. And his brother, too." Pausing, Medici clicked open his briefcase and pulled out a stack of papers. "However, my real and legal name is Gustavo Jakub Klosinski. Which makes your contract with 'Max Medici' not worth the paper it's printed on."

Medici ripped up his copy of the contract with Vandevere, tossing fragments into the air like confetti.

Vandevere's face drained of blood as shock set in.

Medici grinned at him. "Secret to show business, my friend: always leave a monkey in your desk."

"This is fraud," Vandevere railed, finally recovering himself somewhat. "I will sue you."

"Yeah? Well, I'm no expert, but I think you have bigger problems here." Medici nodded to the burning circus behind him.

*Crack. Crack. Boom!* The roller coaster's track, weakened by fire, collapsed in a groan of metal and wood. Vandevere's stomach churned.

"I should have put my money on you, Mr. Lucky Dust," Remington said nearby, nodding at Medici. "Come on, I'll get you a couple hot dogs."

"Sounds good, J. G." Medici smiled, tipped his hat at Vandevere, then walked away with the banker and his associates.

Left alone, Vandevere watched Dreamland burn. Several cops finally hustled him away from the fire, ignoring his protestations that he'd been robbed. As far as the policemen were concerned, the elephant had quit.

# CHAPTER
# TWENTY-FOUR

ew York City scrolled underneath Joe, lines of streets, buildings jabbing upward, and patches of grass here and there. He couldn't believe they were actually flying! Thick metal cables, wooden scaffolding, and buildings cluttered the sky as Dumbo and his passengers neared the docks.

"Whoa, slow down!" Milly cried. "No, speed up," she hurriedly corrected herself.

Joe smiled at his sister's hemming and hawing. She should just relax. Dumbo knew what he was doing.

With a *whoosh*, Dumbo slid between two buildings, but a new obstacle loomed in front.

"Watch where you're headed. Bridge. *Bridge*. Dumbo, BRIDGE!" Milly shrieked.

"Yeah!" Joe pumped his fist as Dumbo veered up, up, up, aiming for the clouds, and zoomed over the towers of the bridge.

As he leveled out, Milly and Joe peered down at the pier and saw the tiny figures—and one not-so-tiny elephant—on it. Flushed with excitement, the kids pointed, but Dumbo needed no guidance. He'd spotted his mother as well.

"*Eeeugh!*" Dumbo trumpeted in answer to his mother's call. But he wasn't used to two passengers. As Milly's and Joe's weight threw him off-balance, Dumbo overcompensated, ears flaring as he came in for a landing, rump down.

*Bump, bump, bump. Crunch.* The young elephant bounced along the pier before digging in his feet and sliding to a stop in the gravelly dirt.

"*Eeeeugh!*" Mrs. Jumbo greeted him, her trunk arching high.

Dumbo wriggled as he stood up and Milly and Joe quickly slid off. Without hesitation, Dumbo galloped toward his mother, and the two nuzzled and squeaked at each other, eyes shining.

Two arms swept Milly and Joe into a hug. "Oh, thank goodness," Colette said. "I was so scared for you." She kissed their cheeks and pulled them in tight. Then she sat back on her heels, her face clouded by a stark realization.

"Where's your father?" Colette asked.

"Don't worry, he'll be here," Milly said confidently.

Right on cue, a whinny pierced the air, followed by the ringing of horseshoes on cobblestones. Holt rounded the corner astride a beautiful horse—right where he belonged.

Relief flooded Holt's chest as he swung down and hugged his children tight. Then a glint of mischief appeared in his eye. He chucked Milly and Joe under the chin one at a time.

"Now see there? What did I tell you? I knew you could ride. You were born to ride," he said.

The kids giggled.

Pramesh stepped forward, Mrs. Jumbo's lead in his hand. He cleared his throat, reluctantly interrupting the family reunion. "Please, we must hurry. The sooner we're in international waters, the safer they'll be."

Suddenly solemn, the group gathered around Dumbo and his mother.

Colette leaned in and kissed Dumbo's forehead. "*Merci*, brave little friend, for showing me how to soar again."

Next was Holt. "Thank you. For everything," he said simply. He couldn't possibly put into words how much Dumbo had taught him, and how grateful he was that this little elephant had brought him and his kids together again as a true family.

"Bye, Dumbo," Joe said, rubbing the elephant's ear. "I don't have any peanuts." He sniffed, holding back tears, then hugged Dumbo around the trunk. He was sad to see the elephants leave; Dumbo's goofy, happy clumsiness had brightened Joe's life. "I'm gonna miss you so much!"

Joe stepped back and tucked himself into Holt's side as Milly knelt next to Dumbo, her eyes bright.

"You'll always be right here," she said, touching her heart.

Dumbo's trunk reached forward, wrapped around her hand, and tugged it to his own body. He nodded at her.

*Huuuuuuuuuhhhn.* The ship's horn blew loudly.

"Last call for cargo—all aboard!" the captain called, waving to the group on the dock.

Holt and his kids dropped back and Pramesh approached Mrs. Jumbo with a sweet smile, pulling a palm leaf from his bag and waving it in front of her.

"This way, great glorious miracles. This way lies paradise," he said, coaxing Mrs. Jumbo up the ramp.

Chuffing, Dumbo rose up off the ground and flapped along beside his mother, doing a few loops around the ramp just for fun. Milly and Joe laughed and joined the rest of Medici's troupe on the pier, all waving as Pramesh, Arav, and the spectacular elephants reached the deck. Crew members pulled up the ramp and cast off from the dock.

*Huuuhn, huuuuhhn!* The SS *Good Hope* reversed away from the pier and turned toward the open sea, slowly fading into the distance. But a large-eared wonder flapped above the deck, waving his trunk one last time before joining his mother at the rail.

Colette dabbed at her eyes, then turned to Holt. "Well, cowboy, there goes our act. So I guess this is goodbye?"

Holt studied her, then held out his hand. "May I?" Smiling up at him, she took it. He pulled her in, dipping his lips to hers.

Breaking off the kiss, he winked at her. "How's that for goodbye?"

She laughed. "In France, we kiss twice," she said, tugging his face back to hers.

Milly and Joe locked gazes, bemused smiles on their faces. This would be the start of a new adventure not just for Dumbo and his mother, but for them as well. Ivan and Catherine came up beside them, then

Miss Atlantis and Puck, Rongo, the acrobats, and the clowns.

Then, to their surprise, they saw Medici coming down the pier toward them.

"Did I miss the send-off?" he asked, peering around for Dumbo and Mrs. Jumbo, though it would have been pretty hard to hide those two.

"How did you know?" Holt said.

"Well, I followed the trail of astonished faces pointing skyward."

"They've gone. Pramesh is taking them home to India, where they belong," Holt said.

Medici nodded. "Ah, well, I'm sorry I didn't get to say bon voyage." Clapping his hands, he rubbed them together and faced his old troupe. "All right, folks. It's great to be back with you again. Sorry about that mess with Vandevere, but he's got nothing on us, so we're free and clear to hit the road again. What do you say?"

A murmur ran through the crowd and several performers crossed their arms.

"Aw, come on, now. Think of all the joy we can bring to people everywhere. I just heard about this fella selling a pair of tigers—"

Rongo stepped forward. "Uh-uh. No tigers. No bears. No elephants. No wild animals. We've been talking, and we think it's time for a new kind of circus."

Medici considered the determined faces before him. "All right then." He shrugged. "No wild animals. Anything else?"

"Actually, yes," Milly said.

Medici grinned as she explained her idea, and then everyone began chiming in with other possible changes to their acts. Joe bit his lip, wondering when to offer his own proposal—he was ready to join his family and friends onstage. The circus director nodded, the excitement and enthusiasm of the group growing with each suggestion. Whatever came next, it would be their show, on their own terms.

# CHAPTER
# TWENTY-FIVE

oplin, Missouri, didn't look much different than it had nine months ago. Winter had come and gone, but the train station, city streets, and empty meadow looked the same. Medici grinned as his team—no, his *family*, for that's what they were—began to unload their new, improved, streamlined circus. No animal pens needed, and just one main tent. He'd been dubious at first they could pull off a circus without animals, but one rehearsal had convinced him otherwise. What better place to premiere their revolutionary new show than the birthplace of Dumbo? Medici only hoped some of that luck

had hung around, because he had a feeling the first night would be crawling with reporters waiting to see what Medici had up his sleeve. They'd find out soon enough.

* * *

Milly carefully placed the circular tin in the center of the wheel she'd constructed. Next to her, Joe's foot jiggled in anticipation.

"Almost ready . . ." Milly leaned over and pressed a picture of her parents on horseback firmly onto the starry backdrop inside the tin.

"Okay, we are cleared for takeoff," Milly said, spinning the wheel.

She and Joe crouched together, peering through the slats in the tin. Before their eyes and along the walls of the tent, Annie and Holt were riding across the night sky, forever together.

"She'll always be part of the show," Holt said from the doorway of the tent.

Milly and Joe made room and Holt joined them. So this was what Milly had been planning with all the publicity photos and flyers she'd been carting around in her bag. He wished he'd never ripped them up, but she'd done a beautiful job of gluing them back together. More impressively, she'd built her very own zoetrope—making it look like the pictures were moving!

"Milly, my dear," Holt said, "you are a marvel."

"Just wait until you see the arm we ordered for you!" Milly said.

"What? You shouldn't have." Holt teared up as Joe slid a box out from beneath his bed.

"Colette helped. She said she wanted her film money to go to a good cause and then mumbled something about you now having no excuse *not* to sweep the floors?" Milly said sweetly.

Opening up the box, Holt gasped. The mechanical arm and hand sparkled. When Milly and Joe helped him strap it on, it fit much more comfortably than the one Medici had given him. With the fingers of his new hand, he grasped a cup and brought it to his mouth. Then he set it back down and reached out for what he wanted to hold most in the world—Milly and Joe. The family embraced as images of Annie and Holt flashed before them.

They could never go back to the past, but the future was coming and it held some amazing miracles. Somewhere, Holt knew, Annie was smiling down at them, and they would always carry her in their hearts.

"You guys ready for tomorrow?" Holt asked.

"You bet!" Joe bounced up and down.

"You're going to knock their socks off, kid," his dad told him. "And Milly, you've done a superb job. I'm so proud of both of you."

* * *

A few hours later, curious crowds began to pour in the gates, moving down the midway, where booths and sideshows lined the path to the main tent. Medici stood on a podium to welcome them, black top hat shining in the lights and the tails of his jacket hanging behind him.

"Ladies and gentlemen," Medici called. "Introducing our world-famous flying elephant!"

*Fwooop!* An air cannon blasted a clown in an elephant costume through the air. He landed on a trampoline and somersaulted away.

Medici smiled, then waved the crowd onward.

"Welcome to the Medici Family Circus—where we believe *no* wild animals should ever be held in captivity."

As he guided the crowd toward the main tent, Medici pointed out the acts.

"Behold Ivan the Wonderful and Catherine the Greater!"

With a flash of smoke, Ivan and Catherine released their doves into the air, their coos a soothing chorus.

312

"See Rongo, the world's strongest and most versatile man!"

From atop his stage, Rongo flexed his biceps, then lifted four acrobats dressed as zebras up on a board. He made it seem as though they were light as feathers, which they were not. Rongo had trained and practiced and honed his skills until he could truly dazzle the audience—no trickery involved.

As some people moved past him, Medici continued. "Then get bewitched by Miss Atlantis, now performing underwater Shakespeare nightly with the world's only merman, Puck!"

Miss Atlantis and Puck waved from the expanded tank, the water trapped in the double-paned glass bubbling up in front of them. They'd written their own adaptation of Shakespeare's plays, arguing long into their evening rehearsals about who'd get the best lines. But together, they'd titled their act *To Breathe or Not to Breathe*. Miss Atlantis flicked her tail against Puck's, and he smiled broadly.

"And visit our newest attraction, Milly Farrier's World of Wonders, to discover all the real-life amazements that are shaping tomorrow today," Medici announced as they reached the tent closest to the main one.

Milly stepped out and waved, hoping people would

come to her modest tent. She didn't have nearly the collection Dreamland's science exhibit had held, but she'd managed to track down quite a few intriguing new inventions and had even made some tweaks of her own to showcase the endless possibilities that lay ahead. She couldn't wait to share the power and beauty of science with everyone.

Drawing the crowd into the main tent, Medici pointed and a pack of clowns clambered into the center ring. They were piled along each other, using their hands to walk on the ground like a many-legged horse as Joe perched on the final one. Joe waved his brand-new cowboy hat around in the air, pretending the clowns were a horse.

"Yee-haw!" he cried.

"Marvel at the skills of the legendary Holt, our cowboy of the future," Medici called out.

The clowns spilled apart, tumbling in all directions, and Joe somersaulted off just as a real stallion thundered into the ring.

Equipped with his new mechanical arm, Holt sat astride the horse, confidently steering it around the ring. Drawing a pistol, he fired at a clump of balloons high in the air, holding a lyra aloft. Swinging from the lyra was Colette, her face aglow in the spotlight as Medici announced her.

"And the pearl of Paris, Colette, Queen of the Heavens!" Medici exclaimed.

*Bang, bang, bang.* As the balloons burst, showering the air with glittering silver confetti, the lyra lowered. Colette flipped through the hoop until she hung from one arm, the other held out gracefully to the side.

She dropped onto the horse's back behind Holt just as they cantered under her.

Amid the hurrahs and clapping, Medici strode out into the center of the ring, flourishing his top hat and baton.

"Yes, meet the mermaids, beasts, and monsters you call freaks and we call family. Young and old, rich or poor, you have a home at our circus. Where anything *is* possible, and miracles happen." He beamed at the audience and winked. "Oh, believe me, they do."

As the show began, the crowd gasped and cheered in delight, their happy voices carrying up into the air past the new, fluttering logo of the Medici Family Circus—a little elephant with wings.

# EPILOGUE
## SOMEWHERE IN THE JUNGLES OF THE INDIAN EMPIRE

trange noises surrounded Dumbo, his ears picking up screeches in octaves he'd never heard and distant growls of what he hoped was thunder. He couldn't hear the rumble of a river, but it definitely smelled as though there were fresh water nearby.

"Eeeee, eeee, eeee!" something cried from the dense greenery.

Dumbo swooped down closer to his mother. What was it? Was it in pain? Were there monsters nearby?

Warmth and calmness radiated off Mrs. Jumbo as Dumbo skimmed the air above her back.

Thwap! As Mrs. Jumbo's ears flapped out, alert, they knocked into Dumbo, sending him off course.

Thump, swish, crunch! Dumbo crashed into the ground and rolled through a tangle of emerald bushes and vines, brown roots and discarded seedpods. Loamy earth filled his nostrils as he stood up and wriggled to free himself of the greenery.

"Eeeuuh." *Mrs. Jumbo's eyes crinkled in amusement and she shook her head at him.*

"Bleeeuugh," *Dumbo replied, spitting out prickly sticks.*

*Angling her ears to the east, Mrs. Jumbo raised her trunk and let out a loud trumpet. Dumbo hopped to her side as they waited. Then, rumbling through the ground, they felt a vibration, followed by the answering bellow of an unfamiliar elephant. Her voice was deep, layered with age and experience, and her tone combined curiosity with caution.*

*Mrs. Jumbo's tail flapped in approval—this stranger sounded like a leader worth following. As she charged forward, Dumbo lifted into the air, weaving around his mother and the trees in excitement. Up ahead, the jungle gave way to a clear patch and the elephants broke from the forest to an amazing sight.*

*They stood on a small cliff overlooking a clear pool of water and a meadow of sweet-scented grasses. Next to the pool, a herd of elephants grazed while their matriarch faced the newcomers. As she and Mrs. Jumbo exchanged greetings, Dumbo hovered a foot off the ground, nervous to display his talents or venture too far from his mother's side.*

*Introductions over, Mrs. Jumbo nudged Dumbo with*

*her trunk. They'd be joining this group.* Go say hello, *she implied.*

*A quiver of anticipation darted over Dumbo's skin. Looking down, he saw two young elephants, perhaps his age, playing in the water. One was resting his front feet on the other's back, trying to push her down in the water, but the second one wrapped her trunk around his back leg and pulled—knocking him over instead. The first got up and splashed water at her. They looked like they were having fun. But what if they didn't like him? Or were afraid of him, like Goliath and Zeppelin?*

*Mrs. Jumbo lowered her head and nuzzled him, as if she knew what he was thinking. Her smile was confident and her stance relaxed. If she trusted them, he would, too.*

*With a few mighty flaps, Dumbo rose higher and then zoomed over the edge of the cliff, down toward the pool below.*

*All the elephants raised their heads and stared as he curled through the air and then dipped lower, trailing his trunk in the water before lifting up again.*

*The two young elephants trotted toward him, their faces confused and awed. They squeaked at him, joyously calling hello, then ran in a circle, inviting him to come play with tails flip-flapping.*

*Joy bubbling inside him, Dumbo flew over, nudged against them, then darted away. One of them reared up and tried to catch hold of his tail.* Ha! *Dumbo thought, veering back and spraying water right in the other elephant's face.*

*He hovered nearby, wondering if that had been rude. He hadn't meant to be rude. But the second elephant was grinning and tossing her trunk in delight as the first spluttered and shook off the droplets. Still dripping, the first elephant bounded over and hauled Dumbo out of the air to tumble into a ball of limbs in the shallow water. The other elephant joined them, piling on top.*

*Mrs. Jumbo, having made her way down the cliff's path, touched her trunk to the matriarch's mouth and then went through the herd, intertwining trunks, flapping ears, and rumbling low to introduce herself to everyone. Reaching the pool, her heart expanded like a flower opening to the sunlight in the morning. Dumbo and his new friends were covered in mud, and the joy on her son's face was everything she'd ever hoped for.*

*They had found their home.*